The Extractor

J.T. Brannan

GREY ARROW PUBLISHING

First published in 2017 by Grey Arrow Publishing

This paperback edition published 2018 by

Grey Arrow Publishing

Copyright © 2017 J.T. Brannan

The moral right of the author has been asserted

This is a work of fiction. Names, characters, places and incidents either are the product of the author's imagination or are used fictitiously, and any resemblance to actual persons, living or dead, businesses, companies, events or locales is entirely coincidental

All rights reserved

ISBN: 978-1980606888

For Jakub and Mia;
and my parents, for their help and support

"These Things We Do,
That Others May Live"
Motto of
US Air Force Pararescue

PROLOGUE

"So, they gonna come through for us, or what?" asked Pete Fletcher, his large frame silhouetted against the dying rays of the evening sun.

Hank Thompson looked across the barren mountaintop at his old friend, checked his watch, and shrugged. Although the man's petulant tone grated, Fletcher had a point. *Was* the Evans family – and in particular, Patrick Evans, the girl's father – going to come through for them?

Thompson damned well hoped so. After all, there was a million dollars riding on this, and that wasn't chicken feed in anyone's book. But time was running out, and there had still been no word about the ransom. Patrick Evans had until midnight to make the cash drop-off, or else Patricia Evans was going to get thrown off the top of this damned mountain; and at this height, the fall would seriously damage those good looks of hers.

The girl was a climber herself, which was how Fletcher and Thompson had come across her in the first place. She'd shown up one day, strutting her stuff in front of the boys; and before long, she'd become one of the group. Funny thing was though, she'd never mentioned who she really was. Who her *daddy* was.

Thompson could understand it, he really could; she'd wanted to be taken on her own merits, as a real person. Only, she'd picked the wrong damn crowd to hang with. Thompson and his boys were climbers, alright; but they were also meth dealers, armed robbers, carjackers, and now they were kidnappers too. When

Brandon Janes, the youngest of their little gang, had spotted a picture of the girl with her father in a local paper, what happened next was a no-brainer. Tricia had been bundled up and thrown in the back of their truck, a safe location had been found, and the ransom notice had been sent out. The work was new to them, but they'd all taken to it pretty naturally.

There were eight of the gang on the mountaintop, with another couple strung out on the road below, in opposite directions, to watch for the cops. Thompson's hacker friends told him that Evans hadn't called the police, but it paid to be sure. They hadn't crossed any state lines anyway, so at least the Feds wouldn't be getting involved.

There were another two of his gang all the way over in Salt Lake City, where the drop-off was supposed to go down; and he hoped he would be hearing from them *real* soon.

Thompson watched as one of his other guys tried to get a bonfire going. "Jules," Thompson hissed across the flat rock, "what the hell are you doing?"

"Damn, Hank," Jules Beddoes said, lighter in hand, "we almost froze our asses off last night, don't you remember?"

Thompson sighed. He was older than the others, he had to remember; some of them still needed a little guidance. "Jules, you dumb sonofabitch – you light a fire up here, it's gonna be seen for a thousand freakin' miles around, are you crazy?"

Jules stopped, looked at his lighter, looked back at

Thompson in disappointment, then slowly nodded his head and put the lighter away. Kid had probably just been smoking too much reefer, Thompson figured. Well, he laughed to himself, maybe they'd all had a bit too much. What kind of crazy-ass idea was it to come up here anyway? Yes, it was pretty secure – you'd have to freeclimb the thing to get up here, and what cops were gonna do that? Thompson and his boys would see them coming from miles away, anyway. But they could easily have just stayed at the house back in Provo, where they'd kept the girl for the past week. And yet, with the deadline approaching, Thompson had got nervous, and brought the girl out here, where he felt safe. Perched atop one of the great sandstone columns of the Courthouse Towers, within Utah's incredible Arches National Park, Thompson felt like a king. But a bonfire would soon draw attention to them, and that was something he *didn't* want.

The girl was being kept in one of the tents they'd set up on the mountaintop, and had been well looked after; or at least, as far as he knew. But some of his guys could have problems keeping their dicks in their pants, he knew, and he supposed there were no guarantees. But she was still alive, and that was the main thing.

It didn't worry him that Tricia would identify them, once the ransom had been paid. After all, with a few hundred grand in his back pocket, he wasn't going to stick around here. No, he'd move on south to Mexico, and maybe Brazil after that. If the boys wanted to come with him, they were welcome. And if they didn't, they could go to hell.

Thompson sighed as the sun finally dipped below the horizon, night falling across the park. He checked his watch – just under four hours to the deadline. Who was he kidding, anyway? There was no way in hell that Tricia was making it off this mountain alive. At the end of the day, what possible sense did it make to leave a living witness?

No, he knew what would happen come midnight – whether the ransom was paid or not, Tricia would die.

John Lee steadied his breath, completely silent as he waited at the base of the huge sandstone tower, fingers tentatively gripping the dark rock in front of him.

It was pitch black out here in the park; it was far enough away from civilization for there to be precious little artificial light, and a dense bank of clouds meant that even the moon and the stars were going to be of no help tonight.

Still, Lee figured as he rested there, attuning his senses, such a situation was already working in his favor. The guys down on the road – hardly concealed, sitting in their pickup trucks – hadn't noticed him as he'd hiked right past them. He'd considered taking them out, but had decided against it – if they were supposed to check-in with the guys at the top of the Courthouse Towers on a regular basis, it could create more problems than it solved.

Finding the gang had been easy; or at least that's what Phoenix De Maio had told him, anyway. Phoenix was a computer whizz, and was responsible for intelligence gathering, hacking, electronic surveillance, and a whole load of other hi-tech stuff that Lee just couldn't get his head around.

He had worked alone for the first missions of his new "career", but when he'd rescued Phoenix – a graduate of MIT, and the daughter of one of France's wealthiest industrialists – from a team of kidnappers in Marseilles, she had begged to help him with his work. He'd reluctantly agreed, and they'd operated side by side ever since, although their relationship often veered away from the strictly professional. Lee was aware that she wanted something more, but – still haunted by memories of what had happened to his own family – he was reluctant to let things go too far.

The fact that she had herself been kidnapped, meant that Phoenix always took these particular missions personally. After their team had received the call from Alexandra Grayson – the ex-sports agent who handled the business side of things for Lee – alerting them to Patricia Evans' abduction and ransom, Phoenix had wasted no time in going to work.

Lee didn't know how she'd done it – and nor did he want to – but within a day of being contacted, she'd located the gang that had taken Patrick Evans' daughter. The only problem was time – Evans hadn't contacted the police, or the Feds, but had left it late in the day before deciding to risk contacting an outside contractor. So, by the time Lee was ready to go, Patricia Evans had already left her prior location in the basement of a house in Provo and had been transported to the top of a sandstone column in the middle of the Utah wilderness.

It tied in with the background of the alleged kidnappers – a nasty little crew led by Hank Thompson, who got their kicks freeclimbing their way around the state when they weren't knocking over diners, burglarizing houses, stealing cars or dealing drugs.

Lee's team had the resources to call in a helicopter for a direct attack on the mountaintop, but such a tactic would do nothing for Patricia's survival – she'd be thrown off the top of the sandstone column as soon as they heard the telltale roar of the rotors.

From Lee's experience of such missions, Patrick Evans had done the right thing by not contacting the cops – far too often, the kidnap victims ended up dead when law enforcement got involved. Lee's success rate, on the other hand, was one hundred percent.

To date, anyway; but he had no intention of letting that percentage slide.

The climb up would be hard, Lee knew. Not only was it pitch black out here in the park, but he was also unable to use conventional equipment. There were pitons already in place – presumably used by Thompson and his boys – but there were no ropes attached, and Lee didn't want to risk the sound of metal on metal from using them. At night, sound seemed to travel a lot further, especially in such an unpopulated area. If they heard him climbing, they might just send Patricia Evans over the side to meet him.

It meant he was going to have to free-solo the

rockface; not an impossible task for a man like him perhaps, but far from an easy one. There *was* a positive side to having no ropes or safety equipment, he told himself as he edged toward the tower; it would make climbing the thing a hell of a lot quicker.

But maybe, he considered as he reached out to grip the rough sandstone in front of him, he should have agreed to the helicopter after all.

Forty minutes later, John Lee was at the lip of the mountaintop, ears straining along with his muscles as he clung to the side of the huge sandstone column and tried to listen for movement nearby.

His team, back at their base on an otherwise uninhabited island in the Bahamas, were constantly trying to make him go hi-tech. Marcus Hartman, his logistics specialist and a former US Army quartermaster, was relentless in his campaign to get Lee to use the most up-to-date gear; but his complaints were nothing compared to those of Yukio Mabuni, Lee's weapons and specialist equipment guru. A former officer in the CIA's Directorate of Science and Technology, Mabuni believed every problem had a technologically-enhanced answer.

Sometimes, Lee gave in and followed their advice; after all, his prior work with the US Air Force's Special Tactics Unit ensured that he was well aware of what capabilities were out there, and how to use most of it.

But – at this stage in his life – John Lee had gone back to basics. Hartman could use all of the technology he wanted to get Lee to where he needed to be, along with his gear; and Mabuni could provide him with modern versions of tried-and-trusted – and sometimes ancient – weapons and equipment; but when it got down to the nitty-gritty, face-to-face stuff, Lee wanted to keep things old-school. He'd tried the modern way, and it wasn't for him.

Mabuni, for his part, still had a hard time accepting that Lee didn't kill people. Not anymore, anyway; his past had left him scarred, and he had vowed never to kill again. The weapons he demanded from Mabuni, therefore, were all non-lethal, which seemed to give the ex-CIA man a constant headache. But it was a vow that Lee intended never to break, and one that set him apart from his competitors in the "extraction" business.

Hastings, Inc., for example, was a case in point; Matt Hastings, its infamous CEO, had no moral qualms about ordering his men to do whatever it took to complete the task they were being paid for, and he had an army of lawyers ready and waiting to deal with the aftermath. They were the Apple of the extraction world, the top player in the corporate market. Lee's own outfit was rather less well-known, and for good reason – Lee himself was still wanted by the US military for allegedly going AWOL. It wasn't strictly true – Lee had asked to resign after his last disastrous, psychically-damaging mission in Iraq, but had been refused – but he was still a figure of some controversy. The CIA had spread damaging rumors about him, and nobody knew what to believe. The military, the intelligence services and the government said one thing – that he was a deserter of the worst sort – while the popular press, aided by the constant work of Alexandra Greyson, said quite another. While some denounced him as a traitor, others hailed him as a hero.

Like most things in life, Lee knew that the truth might well be found somewhere in the middle.

He breathed out, low and quiet, centering himself for what lay ahead.

This, he supposed, was the hero part.

There were four lookouts, each one stationed at a side of the column that coordinated with the points of the compass.

Light discipline was surprisingly good, Lee saw; but there were occasional flashes from cellphone screens, and a couple of the gang were even smoking. Lee recognized the sickly-sweet smell of marijuana, which tied into what he'd heard about the men.

Lee knew that the light from the smokes, and looking into those cellphone screens, for however little time, would ruin the men's night vision. Lee's, however, was operating perfectly. Before setting out on his hike across the desert, he'd taken herbal concoctions designed to improve the eyes' sensitivity to light, and then used the first couple of hours of darkness to grow accustomed to it, adjusting his senses to the conditions until he could see almost as well as during the day. Well, he admitted, maybe that was overstating the case; but he could see well enough, and that was all that mattered.

Mabuni, of course, recommended that he wear the latest night vision goggles, but they reminded Lee too much of his time in the military, the later years of which he was trying very hard to forget. Besides which, he'd always found the NVGs to damage depth perception to an unacceptable degree. It was fine for shooting at medium range, but when things went hand-to-hand – as they now often did, since he had foresworn the use of guns – the goggles could be a liability.

Lee lay on the cold stone floor, just twenty feet away from the nearest guy, who was stood at the edge, staring out toward the east. He silently withdrew the slender blowpipe from his combat vest, placed his lips over the end, aimed, and blew.

Lee watched as the man's hand went to the back of his neck, where the poisoned needle had struck, then he was up and moving fast across the mountaintop, catching the body as it collapsed and easing it silently down to the ground.

He crawled along the edge of the sandstone tower, taking out another two sentries in the same fashion – get close, aim the blowpipe, fire, run and catch.

The darts weren't fatal, the poison mild – enough to induce unconsciousness but far from death.

Lee saw that there was a tent in the middle of the rocky expanse that made up the peak of the sandstone column, and he knew that was where the girl would be. Four more men were stationed outside, and Lee could see that Hank Thompson was one of them, recognizing him from photos provided by Phoenix. The guy was constantly checking his cellphone, presumably waiting for the call from Salt Lake to tell him the ransom had been paid, and he was a rich man.

Lee wasn't sure about the second guy, right next to Thompson, but thought it might be Pete Fletcher, the leader's right-hand man, and a thoroughly nasty piece of work. His jacket included charges of robbery, rape, aggravated assault and manslaughter. A violent man, and one Lee would have to be careful with.

The other two were facing away from him, and Lee couldn't make them out. They were talking in low whispers, which carried across the barren mountaintop.

"They gonna call, do ya think?" one of the men with his back to Lee asked, anxiety heavy in the whispered voice.

"They'll call," Hank responded. "One way or another, at least."

"But what if they don't pay?" asked the fourth man. "What are we gonna do, are we really gonna kill her, are we –"

"What the hell else do you think we're gonna do?" Fletcher said gruffly. "She's seen our faces, and kidnap's a hardcore deal, we'll be goin' down for life, you get it? Whether we get the money or not, there's no freakin' way we're lettin' her walk, you got that?" He spat on the floor. "I'll throw the bitch off the mountain myself."

Lee knew there was less than an hour until the deadline, and he had no doubts that someone in the group would do as promised, whether the ransom was paid or not – if not Thompson himself, then Fletcher for sure.

That left Lee plenty of time to get to the girl though.

But first things first, Lee told himself as he edged across the dark mountaintop toward the fourth sentry. Take out the outer perimeter first, before moving inward.

Tommy Conway was bored. What the hell were they doing out here, anyway? They'd had a sweet deal going back at the house; nobody was gonna bother them there, with the rich bitch stashed down in the basement. They'd never got caught there selling meth, and they'd been doing that for years, why would anyone have come down there to find the girl?

But Hank had got a bug up his ass about being discovered, and demanded they all take a ride out here. It wasn't that Tommy didn't like it out on the towers; quite the opposite, he was a climbing freak, he loved to be out there, doing what he did best. Only they'd normally have a fire going, music playing loud, beer flowing freely . . . but Hank was having none of that stuff. It was all business. But at least he could still smoke his pot, Tommy considered as he drew in a lungful and breathed it out into the cool night air.

Yeah, at least he still had his pot.

He took another drag and asked himself what good he was doing there, looking out over the southern edge of the tower. They'd be able to see headlamps from miles away, and who the hell was gonna climb this thing in the dark anyway?

But Hank was wary about choppers, worried that the mountaintop could be hit by some sort of aerial assault. But that was nonsense too, and Tommy knew it. After all, how the hell would anyone even know they were out here? It was probably just paranoia, from all the shermsticks Hank had been smoking. Just wound some people up that way, he guessed.

But dammit, why did he have to waste his time staring out into space? He threw the butt of his reefer onto the floor and ground it up with the heel of his climbing shoe, decided he was gonna have a little word with Hank Thompson, and turned back toward –

What the hell?!

He felt something pass by his face, so close it nearly touched him, a waft of hot air like the passage of a bullet. But there was no sound, nothing at all, and he opened his mouth to shout a warning to the others when a shadow emerged from the darkness, racing straight toward him . . .

Lee couldn't believe his bad luck, the guy turning like that at just the wrong moment, the dart missing him by mere millimeters. He had more darts, but no time to load another into the pipe before the guy started shouting, and Lee was on his feet before his conscious mind had even made the decision, the long, black-carbonized chain appearing in his hands as he ran, closing the distance quickly, releasing the chain . . .

The metal links whipped out toward the startled

man, the end wrapping itself around his neck, choking his calls for help before they could leave his throat. The guy's hands reflexively reached for the chain around his neck, but it was too little, too late; Lee wrenched him forward by the chain and connected with a heavy right hand to the guy's jaw, dropping him instantly.

Lee used the chain to slow the man's fall, careful at the same time not to break his neck by doing it, loosening the hold with a practiced flick of his wrist.

He turned quickly to the center of the mountaintop, seeing the faint outline of the group of figures some fifty yards distant, clustered around the tent.

But something was wrong, they weren't just chatting anymore, they were turning this way, staring, pointing . . .

Hank Thompson's eyes snapped toward the southern edge of the tower, though he didn't know why . . . was it a sound of some kind he'd heard? Something metal . . .?

"Did anyone hear that?" he whispered to the others, eyes straining to pierce the darkness. Dammit, he couldn't see anything, why had he been staring into that damn cellphone all night?

"Hear what?" Fletcher said, his head turning to stare southward like Thompson.

"Don't know," Thompson murmured, a bad feeling creeping up through him as he looked around at the rest of the mountaintop, from south to north, and from east to west. He still couldn't see a damn thing, anywhere. "Tommy?" he called out, drawing his Colt .45 before the kid even had a chance to answer, already knowing deep down that something was desperately wrong here. "Connor?" he called out to the east, when Tommy didn't answer, nodding at his other boys to draw their guns. "Lee?" he shouted to the west. "Brad?" to the south.

Nothing, from any of them. He slid the safety off, his finger caressing the trigger.

"Get the girl," he told Fletcher; and even in the darkness, he could see his old friend smile as he nodded and headed into Patricia Evans' tent.

John Lee knew that he could sprint in a straight line across the mountaintop and reach the four men in under six seconds, perhaps even before they had time to fully react. And yet he could see that Thompson was already drawing his gun, staring toward where Lee had dropped the fourth unconscious body.

And so, instead of racing straight ahead, Lee moved fast in a semicircle, using the dark and the shadows as his friends, knowing that they would never see him. They might hear him though, he realized, and he moderated his speed, careful not to crash into the rocks underfoot. The soft-rubber-soled climbing shoes he wore helped too, and he covered the distance in near silence.

He was still twenty feet away when Fletcher entered the tent, what looked like a hunting knife in his hand; the other three men were still outside the tent,

Thompson with a handgun, another with a sawn-off shotgun, the third with what looked like an Ingram MAC-10 machine pistol, beloved of street thugs for decades. They were looking around the mountaintop in something close to panic, and Lee knew why – nobody liked the feeling of being stalked from the shadows, of not knowing what was coming to get them. Or *who*.

But then Thompson started shooting, the panic getting to him, firing wildly in every direction, and then the guy with the shotgun was firing too, then the machine pistol opened up, spraying its bullets across the mountaintop at an uncontrollable fifteen hundred rounds per minute.

Lee threw himself to the ground to avoid the gunfire, while keeping his forward momentum going by crawling low across the rockface, eyes averted from the muzzle flashes that would have destroyed his night vision.

And then he was there, right in front of them, without them even realizing, their night vision annihilated by their own gunfire, and he saw that the MAC-10 had locked empty, the rounds all spent; and in the next instant, Lee leaped to his feet and slammed a hard front kick into the man's chest, blasting him six feet back across the rockface.

Lee took note of the position of the other two men and let his body turn in a graceful pirouette, before unleashing a whip-like spinning kick toward the guy holding the shotgun, his heel connecting with the man's head before he could get the weapon around. The contact would have been better with a proper combat boot, but it was still enough to knock the man instantly unconscious.

Lee sensed, rather than saw, the big Colt .45 of Hank Thompson turning his way, and he pounced forward, gripping the gun-arm at the elbow and turning it away; Thompson pulled the trigger, but the powerful round discharged harmlessly into the sandstone floor, even as Lee's open palm smashed the gang leader in the face, shattering his nose. Lee's other hand crossed over to the man's right wrist then, the one that had been gripping the elbow shifting to join it, grabbing and twisting it violently, Thompson screaming as the wrist was broken, the big Colt falling to the ground. Lee sensed that, despite the pain the man was in, he was aiming to throw a punch with his undamaged hand, and Lee took the advantage and threw a short kick up into Thompson's balls, before smashing an elbow into the side of his head. Thompson's eyes rolled up into his head and he dropped unconscious to the floor, all three men taken out in a matter of seconds.

But those seconds were enough for Fletcher to have dragged Patricia Evans out of the tent, jagged hunting knife up at her throat as he dragged her toward the edge of the tower. Even in the cloudy darkness, Lee could see the violence in Fletcher's eyes, the resolution to do whatever was necessary to win; or at least, to survive.

"Whoever's out there," Fletcher snarled, "you better back away from me, right now! Right now, or else

I do the bitch, I'll slit her freakin' throat wide open! I –"

His words turned to a violent yell of pain as a dull black shuriken throwing star lodged itself into his hand, causing his fingers to spasm and open, the hunting knife falling to the rocky ground beneath him.

But Fletcher was close to the edge now, and Lee watched in mounting horror as the man pulled the girl, who was screaming now for all she was worth, toward him, obviously with the intention of throwing her right off the mountain.

Lee was in motion instantly, covering the distance between them in the blink of an eye, his body colliding with Fletcher's and knocking Patricia out of the way, even as the momentum of the two men took them both toward the edge, closer, closer . . .

And then over, into the inky blackness below.

Lee felt himself travelling into the ether, unconnected to anything except the body of the other man, holding each other in a wrestler's embrace as they plummeted to the earth beneath them.

But Lee felt one of his hands reach out, as if of its own accord, his vice-like fingers touching, then grasping the rockface, digging deep, clenching, gripping; and a moment later, he felt his descent arrest fully, a wrenching pain tearing through his shoulder. The shock of the sudden stop tore Fletcher from the embrace, and Lee ignored the pain as he reached out with his other hand instinctively to grab for the man's still-falling body, unwilling to see him die.

Lee's hand grasped Fletcher's wrist, and hauled him back up, so that the man could grab hold of the rockface himself. He watched in the dark, trying not to think about the hundreds of feet of empty space beneath them, as Fletcher's hands latched onto the sandstone, the toes in his specialist climbing boots digging in moments later.

Lee took in their situation quickly, saw that they were a good ten feet below the lip of the mountaintop; and he was just about to start climbing back up, when his peripheral vision caught sight of a small blade arcing toward him.

He lifted an arm to deflect the blow, surprised that Fletcher was able to operate so fast; he'd seen the hunting knife fall to the ground after the shuriken had hit the man's hand, so the blade must be a new one, drawn and used in one fluid action, even as Fletcher had taken his grip on the rockface. Lee had to admire the man's tenacity, even as he knocked the knife-arm to the side and slammed a callused fist into his face.

But it wasn't enough to take the man out, and the knife was soon swinging back toward Lee; only this time, Lee didn't deflect the attack, but instead reared back out of the way, gripping tight to the rock as the blade swiped past him and lashing up with one of his booted feet to the underside of Fletcher's jaw.

The strike connected hard, whipping the man's head back violently and causing him to lose his grip on the sandstone tower completely, and Lee watched in mute horror as Fletcher's body sailed away into the night.

And then, for the second time in as many minutes, Lee himself was tumbling through the air as he threw himself after Fletcher, one hand reaching out to grab the man by the ankle of his pants while the other scraped down the side of the tower, before his fingers closed around a barely discernable outcrop, gripping tight and holding them secure.

Lee breathed out slowly, once again ignoring the renewed pain in his shoulder, as Fletcher's body swung back and forth in the dark night beneath him.

Damn, Lee thought as he looked back up toward the top, now twenty feet away. Now he was going to have to haul this sonofabitch all the way back up there.

Less than five minutes later, Lee was back on the top of the tower, the unconscious body of Pete Fletcher laid out alongside the others – all now bound and cuffed, the arms of a deliriously grateful Patricia Evans wrapped around him.

"It's okay," he said, hugging her back, knowing only too well what she must have gone through. "It's okay."

She held him close for a long time, before breaking away and looking out over the mountainside. "I don't know how to thank you," she said breathlessly. "I really don't."

"Thank your father," Lee said. "He hired me."

Patricia nodded and smiled, then looked back out over the mountainside. "But . . . how are we gonna get down from here?"

Lee smiled in the dark, and pulled out his cellphone, dialing a familiar number.

"You want the chopper now?" the guttural tones of Marcus Hartman asked over the crystal-clear connection.

"You got it," Lee confirmed. "Send it over, okay?"

Lee wasn't a big fan of technology, but he had to admit, it sure as hell beat hauling eight men and a woman off the mountain by himself.

"Yes, sir," Hartman said. "It's on its way. See you back in the Caribbean, my friend."

The blades of the chopper could be heard just minutes later, and a smile covered Lee's face for the first time that evening. The mission had been a success; the girl had been rescued and – once he'd dropped these sonsofbitches off with the local cops – he'd finally be on his way home.

PART ONE

Chapter One

"I'm glad you're back," Phoenix said happily, putting her arms around John Lee and kissing his cheek. She was going for the lips, but she felt his resistance and changed at the last moment. She was so glad to see him, and yet deflated at the same time; he was still cold toward her, unwilling – perhaps unable – to reciprocate the feelings she had for him.

And yet they *had* been close before, been lovers more than once, since John had rescued her and they'd started working together. But he'd always been so conflicted, like he'd wanted to be there with her but at the same time felt that he didn't deserve to be.

She knew he'd been married once, had had a little girl too; and she was also one of the few people in the world who knew what had happened to them. Something like that, she thought sadly, how could it fail to affect him? It was a long time ago now, but some wounds just didn't heal as well as others. And he'd told her many times that he felt strongly for her, might even love her, but was scared to commit, to endanger her.

She couldn't blame him, not really . . . and yet when

he flinched as she'd tried to kiss him, she couldn't help but feel a terrible emptiness inside.

"I'm glad to *be* back," John said to her, holding her by the shoulders and leveling his gaze with hers. "I missed you."

Phoenix felt her heart leap in her chest, and yet when John leaned in to kiss her, it was still just on the cheek.

Lee wanted to kiss her on the lips, wanted to hold her, embrace her, even to carry her up to his room and make love to her, then lie there with her in his arms and talk to her for hours, and yet . . .

Why couldn't he do it?

Helena and Anabelle had been gone for years now, and there was no bringing them back, so why couldn't he let go? And yet it wasn't that simple. He couldn't afford to let anyone close to him, couldn't let anyone use Phoenix to get to him. It was bad enough that they worked together, but he knew that if they entered into a full relationship, then people could use her to get to him. And Heaven only knew, there were plenty of people out there who wanted to get to him.

Even if you discounted all of the people whose criminal livelihoods he had destroyed since starting his extraction business, there was still that psycho Brad Thompson from the CIA, the guy who'd recruited him into the Special Activities Division before refusing his resignation just a few short and painful months later; there was the terrorist group from that same damn war which still had a death warrant out on him; and there was an entire Triad group that wanted him dead, in a feud that went back nearly two decades. And that was just the ones he *knew* about.

No, he thought sadly, being too closely associated with him was a recipe for disaster; as painful as it was, he was best off keeping his distance from Phoenix, best off keeping things professional.

At least, he thought in satisfaction, things were fairly safe here on the island. It was a short trip out by boat to Nassau, a quick hop across the Caribbean to Miami and the US mainland, but the place was pretty remote, and hardly anyone knew it was inhabited.

Mabuni had also set up radar and sonar sensors everywhere, and was plugged into the mainframes of most of the world's intelligence and law enforcement agencies. If anyone came for them, they'd know about it well in advance. It wouldn't, Lee promised himself, be like that monastery in Tibet – yet another episode in his life he was trying to forget.

He supposed that was why he was always so keen to be out there on a mission – it helped him forget his past, and all the bad things that it held.

Not that headquarters was a bad place to spend his downtime, Lee told himself as he watched the crystal azure waters gently lapping the soft white sand of the beach he and Phoenix stood on, the speedboat he'd piloted from Miami standing at a floating pontoon just twenty yards away. The temperature was in the high eighties, the sun a flaming ball in a perfect blue sky.

Yes, he considered as he followed the shapely form of Phoenix toward the main house, where lunch was being prepared for them by the live-in chef, life on the island wasn't too bad at all.

"So, the new NVGs work well, John?" Mabuni asked as he sipped at his glass of Mouton Rothschild.

There were four of them around the table, set on a high verandah overlooking the Caribbean. Lee, Phoenix, Mabuni and Hartman celebrated their latest success with lobster and wine, although Lee forewent the alcohol and kept to mineral water. Part of it was for health, but the main reason was that he'd given up drinking when he'd entered a Buddhist temple in northern Thailand, not long after he'd lost his wife. He took a sip of his water, thinking about his mother all those years ago, back in Hong Kong.

She'd always tried to lead him down the Buddhist path, even when they'd moved to Washington, DC with his father's work – and then three years later to the Philippines, then on to South Korea, Japan and China after that. His father had been an American diplomat and they'd been stationed in US embassies around the world, always attending Christian mass to placate the people back home who didn't like their diplomats to follow "foreign religions". His father, for his part, had been of a similar mind; but he'd always let his wife follow whatever faith she wanted to – in private, of course.

Back then, however, Lee had had no real interest in

religion of any kind – Buddhism, Christianity, Hinduism, Islam, they were all boring as far as the young John Lee was concerned. It was physical activity that interested him, and everywhere he went, he begged and cajoled his father into using his contacts to get him the best tuition available – swimming, diving, athletics, gymnastics, fencing, horseback riding, shooting, skiing, snowboarding, free-running, even skydiving, he did them all. At school, he was on the teams for football, soccer and basketball, but always felt more closely tied to those individual pursuits.

And then there were the martial arts, where his real passions lay. In Manila, he had learned Escrima and Kali, then Taekwondo and Hapkido in Seoul, before studying Karate, Judo, Aikido, and even a little Ninjutsu in Tokyo. And when he'd gone to Beijing in his teens, he'd been accepted at one of the top Wu Shu schools, where his skills had been accelerated to the next level. It was there, in fact, that he'd been spotted by a film producer for one of the big Hong Kong movie studios, invited to be part of their experienced and highly-respected stunt team. And that was where . . .

"John?" Mabuni asked. "You listening, man?"

Lee's head cleared in an instant, and he turned to his old friend. "Yeah," he said, "sorry about that, guess I zoned out for a while. What did you say?"

"I *said*," Mabuni sighed, "did you use those NVGs I couriered out to you? The latest thing, the Tier One boys are raving about them, what did you think?"

"I . . . ah . . ."

"He didn't use them," Hartman said with a knowing smile as he gulped down half a glass of wine, "did you, John?"

"Come off it," Mabuni said, shaking his head. "He's gotta have used them, only a freakin' lunatic would go and climb a mountain and take on eight guys in the pitch black, when he's got the best – and I mean the *best* – night vision gear in the business with him. Go on, John," he said, "tell him, why don't you?"

"Look," Lee began sheepishly, "it might be that those goggles were . . . how do I put this . . . forgotten?"

Mabuni put down his glass and glowered at Lee across the table. "What was that?" he asked, digging a finger theatrically into one of his ears. "Must be my age, maybe the hearing's going a bit, I don't know. I thought you said you *forgot* them?"

Lee shrugged, trying to ignore the look of satisfaction on Hartman's face at being proved right. "I'm sorry Yukio. You know how I am, though."

"Yeah," Mabuni said, "you're an ingrate who doesn't know the value of what he's been given!"

Lee smiled, not angry at his friend's remarks; he knew this was just a bit of friendly jibing, and played along.

"You're just disappointed you don't have a full action report on them," Lee said, "so you can get a few more hits on those geeky review websites of yours."

"Geeky?" Mabuni shot back. "Geeky? My friend, those sites I run are first-class, and you know it."

"I've never looked at them," Lee said with a smile.

"Too geeky for me."

Mabuni picked up a bread roll and hurled it across the table at Lee, a look of mock-indignation across his face; Lee merely raised a hand, caught the roll, and took a bite out of it.

"Careful, John," Hartman said jovially, "you don't want those carbs to ruin that movie-star physique of yours."

"You're talking to a guy who's half-Chinese," Lee said, chewing on more of the roll. "We live on carbs. You ever heard of rice?"

"He's got you there, Marcus," Phoenix said with a little laugh, joining in the conversation for the first time. Lee had been wondering why she'd been so quiet, and figured she'd probably been dwelling on their earlier conversation, and his refusal to enter into a proper relationship with her. He decided he'd definitely have to do some exercise that afternoon; he'd just returned from an operation, and perhaps deserved a day off, but thought it would be a good way of avoiding any more conversations about things he didn't want to discuss.

The island was set up with all the recreational and training facilities Lee would ever need. There was a fully-equipped weights room, a martial arts dojo, a multitude of specially-designed climbing walls, and a full range of gymnastic equipment, not to mention all of the water-sports activities that their location made possible, nearly all year round.

He was just deciding what he'd like to do – maybe an ocean swim to wash away the dust of the desert –

when his cellphone rang.

He answered, only to hear the brash, confident tones of Alexander Grayson on the other end. With so many people hell-bent on taking Lee out of the picture, in one way or another, he didn't involve himself in the public side of the business. Instead, he left it all to Grayson, who had worked first as a journalist, PR guru and social media expert, before becoming an agent to the stars. She'd worked with many of the biggest name in sport and entertainment over the years, before she'd taken on Lee and his extraction business as a client.

It had hurt her in some quarters, with some still wishing to believe that Lee was a traitor, but Grayson wasn't the kind of person to let a few bigoted thugs stand in her way. Lee's business was out of her normal sphere of operations, but he had rescued the children of a valuable client, and she had seen the results of his work first-hand. Appalled at his treatment, she had come to him, offering her services as a go-between; and Lee – seeing the advantages this might have – had agreed without putting up too much of a fight. And so now Grayson dealt with the day-to-day running of the business, including screening all of the potential clients to avoid false-flag jobs designed to lure Lee into a trap. The CIA and the Triads had both tried it before, and each attempt had been only narrowly avoided. Lee was glad to have Grayson in his corner.

"Alex," he said happily, "how are you?"

"Great, John, great. Great work in Utah, Mr. Evans was over the damn moon about it, he really was."

"He paid the second half already?" Lee asked with half a smile. Most contractors in his business wanted the full amount up front, but Lee split it into two payments, with the second due only on successful completion of the mission. Grayson complained, but his confidence was well-placed – he'd never failed to collect the full amount so far. But they normally didn't pay this quickly, and Lee was pleasantly surprised.

"He has," Grayson said, "but that's not why I'm calling."

"Oh?" Lee said, heart leaping ever so slightly in his chest. "What is it?"

"Another job," she said, and the feeling in Lee's chest was confirmed. It looked like he wasn't going to have to hit the gym to avoid difficult discussions with Phoenix after all.

"Tell me about it," he said.

"Well," Grayson told him, "this time, it's something you can really get your teeth into."

Chapter Two

The President of the University of Chicago looked across the large desk at Lee, over the tops of his horn-rimmed spectacles. Greg Dunford was a kindly-looking older gentleman, although perhaps not quite as old as the spectacles, the corded slacks and the tweed jacket made him appear.

"I'm extremely glad that you could make it," he said; and although he appeared genuinely pleased that Lee was there, he also seemed deeply troubled at the same time, as did the other two people seated nearby.

Tom Bakula was the Dean of the Biological Sciences Division, an earnest though frazzled-looking guy in his late-forties, while Sylvia Darrow – younger, and much better-looking in Lee's humble opinion – was a professor within that division's Immunology Faculty.

It wasn't normal practice for him to meet his clients directly anymore, and yet Grayson thought that in this instance, it might be useful. The job seemed more complicated than the usual rescue mission, and she thought he might want to hear it straight from the horse's mouth – or in this case, *mouths*. She'd done her research and it all seemed to be on the level, but Lee had run a series of counter-surveillance routes before entering the hallowed halls of the university itself. He hadn't detected any threat, but he was still alert as he sat there in the opulent, wood-paneled office. He didn't think an attack was likely, but it always paid to be sure.

"And thanks for getting here so quickly," Sylvia Darrow added. "It means a lot to us."

"I'll make it unanimous," Bakula said. "Thank you."

"It's not a problem," Lee said. "Sorry I didn't use the car you sent for me." He'd taken the chopper to Miami, where he'd boarded a private jet to O'Hare. Dunford had sent a limousine to pick him up from the airport, and whisk him to the offices on South Ellis Avenue, but the last thing Lee had wanted to do was get into a strange vehicle, before he'd checked out whether this was properly above-board. He'd chosen a taxi instead, and then reconnoitered the area on foot before the meeting.

"We understand," Dunford said. "Ms. Grayson said you would be unlikely to accept the ride, but we had to make the offer."

The door opened then, and drinks were brought in on a tray by a young man, a wide smile on his face. It was clear that, whatever it was that troubled the three staff members around the table, this man knew nothing about it.

Lee accepted his green tea with thanks, while the others waited as coffee was poured for them from a silver pot. The man smiled again and left, leaving them alone once more.

"So," Lee said as he took a sip of the bitter tea, "who wants to tell me what this is about?"

Lee watched as nervous looks were exchanged, before the president decided to take the lead. "Mr. Lee," he began, "before we tell you what has happened, I would stress that some of what you will hear is – well, we're not the government, it's not *classified* exactly, but–"

"You'd rather I don't speak a word of it to anyone," Lee said, finding the words for him.

"Yes," Dunford said. "Exactly. We are a private research university, and we stand or fall on that research. If we have a lead in something, we prefer to keep it."

"You have my word," Lee said solemnly. "Outside of my team, I won't say anything about this to anyone."

"And your team," Bakula said, "they can be trusted?"

"Absolutely," Lee confirmed.

"Okay," Dunford said, "I'm glad you understand. I hate to act all heavy, but you know how it is. Some things need protecting."

"It's fine, believe me. Now, what's the problem?"

"A research team has gone missing," Darrow answered, to Dunford's surprise, although he seemed happy to let her talk. "*My* research team."

"Missing where?"

"The Amazon rainforest."

"That's a big place," Lee said. "Have you got anything more specific?"

"We have GPS coordinates for their last known location, from the last time they contacted us."

"And when was that?"

"A week ago," Darrow said.

"You haven't heard anything at all from them for a week?" Lee asked, wondering what his chances were of keeping his one hundred percent record.

"Nothing at all," Dunford said gravely. "Of course, we've reported this to the local police, as well as to our own embassy in Brazil, but there's a limit to what they can do. The team were not exactly in the main tourist areas, let's say. The places they were going, maps don't even exist for."

"Okay, but a rescue operation *has* been launched by the locals?"

"Yeah," Darrow said, "as far as we know, although our contact there tells us they're not really doing a hell of a lot."

"So, we didn't know what to do," Dunford said, "but then Tom remembered reading about you in the papers, and we thought, what do we have to lose? You're a specialist in retrieving people from the most dangerous and inhospitable places in the world, from what I gather."

Lee nodded. That was his specialty, and had been since joining the Air Force and being convinced to try out for "superman school", the hardcore, ultimate assessment center that selected men to become PJs – Pararescue Jumpers, the elite of the elite. The unit was formed to help rescue downed pilots from enemy territory during World War II – although its antecedents went all the way back to 1922 – and had also been trained in search and rescue for NASA astronauts in the 1960s. But it was really during the Vietnam War that the PJs had really come into their own, rescuing thousands of pilots who had crash-landed into the forbidding jungles of Vietnam, Laos and Cambodia. Lee had been trained to parachute, fast-rope or SCUBA-dive into anywhere on earth in order to rescue his military brothers and sisters, and had now brought those skills to the open market. Dunford was right – if anyone was right for this job, it was John Lee, "the Extractor", as the press had helpfully dubbed him.

"That's right," Lee said. "That's what I do, and it's why I'm here. But now I need to know why that team is where *they* are. What were they doing in the rainforest?"

There were nervous looks around the table again, and several furtive sips of hot coffee.

"Well," Dunford said, "this is where it gets 'classified', okay?" He had some more coffee, then sighed. "A few months back, we caught wind of a report coming out from Brazil that there was a tribe there, in the Amazon, whose members were resistant to disease."

"You've got to be kidding me," Lee said in disbelief. "That's fairytale stuff, right?"

"We thought there might be some truth in it," Bakula said, a little defensively. "The report was as genuine as you could expect, being about a non-contacted tribe."

"If it's non-contacted, how could there be a report at all?" Lee queried. He'd heard about the presence of such tribes in the rainforest, and knew the Brazilian government were trying to record their existence, and presence, by flying low over vast areas in small airplanes; but if nobody had made contact with this tribe, how in the hell would anyone know that its members were resistant to disease?

"Non-contacted by the 'developed' world," Bakula explained. "The report comes from interviews with members of other tribes in the general area that *have* been contacted."

"And they mentioned this hidden tribe, miraculously immune to disease?" Lee asked skeptically.

"Yes," the president confirmed, "there are three separate groups – none of whom have had any significant contact with one another, I might add – that all tell remarkably similar stories about this one particular tribe."

"And where did this report originate?" Lee asked.

"A professor with FUNAI – that's the Brazilian government's National Indian Foundation – who's one of the main researchers into these tribes. He was supposed to turn the report over to the government, but when he found out about this hidden tribe, he started to have doubts."

"Doubts?"

"Well, concerns that the information wouldn't be

handled in the correct way. In a *moral* way. He was suspicious of some of the people in the government, I guess. Put two and two together – if there were people immune to disease, there might be money to be made."

Lee understood perfectly – if the tribe was real, then everyone would want their little piece of it, including the government. "But he trusted you?"

"He did his doctorate here in Chicago," Dunford answered. "And as far as he would trust anyone with such knowledge, then yes – he trusted us."

"I still don't get it," Lee said. "I thought one of the things about these tribes is that because they haven't had any contact with the outside world, there's been no chance to pick-up any immunity to these 'outside' diseases."

He wasn't an historian, scientist or doctor, but Lee remembered learning about how the invading Europeans with their African slaves had decimated the population of the Americas – in some areas by up to ninety percent – by bringing their diseases with them; diseases to which the indigenous people had no prior exposure or resistance. Smallpox alone had apparently killed millions.

Darrow nodded her head. "That's right," she agreed readily, "and that's one of the things that makes it all so exciting. You see, some of the tribes that claim to have met this unknown group *have* been contacted, and *have* contracted some of the illnesses and diseases of the outsiders they met. Only when they then crossed paths with these people, they didn't pass these on to them."

"You see," Bakula added, "whenever these tribes have met outsiders in the past, the results are often ugly – colds and flu are real problems, and they typically have little or no immunological defenses."

"But your magical tribe *does* have such defenses," Lee commented.

"That's what we think," Darrow said, "and if it's true, then can you imagine what that would mean? It would mean that they don't get their immunity from prior exposure and a build-up of a protective response, but that's it's entirely natural – either genetic, or from something that's a part of their diet. In fact, some of the indicators are that the immunity is linked to long-term ingestion of a certain kind of plant, that grows locally in their area. And that's something we just had to investigate."

"What were you planning on doing if you found them?" Lee asked. "Rounding them up and shipping them back here to your laboratories?"

"Look, Mr. Lee," Darrow said, her tone hardening slightly, "that's not the sort of people we are." She gestured around the room with her hand. "Not the sort of place this is, okay? No, our plan was to try and investigate on the ground, see what we could find out, what data we could collect. Perhaps identify this plant – or flower, or whatever it is – if it exists, collect samples, and bring them back here for analysis."

"And then they'd just be left alone?" Lee asked doubtfully.

Dunford put his coffee cup down and looked across the table at Lee, eyes glinting. "Mr. Lee," he began, "you are a man of the world, I am sure. You are familiar with the realities of life. The report has been written. The news about this tribe will get out, one way or another, if it hasn't already, that's just how these things work. We hoped to be the first ones there, to make contact and then – using Professor Guzman and his contacts at FUNAI – to bring the tribe across the border and into a protected area."

"Across the border?" Lee asked with a raised eyebrow.

"Well, we have reason to believe that the tribe might actually be located on the Peruvian side, which is a bit wilder, a bit more . . . lawless, let's say."

"Illegal loggers," Darrow added, "drug traffickers, coca farmers, they all use the area, vast as it is. The tribe – if it exists – is in danger, even if they don't know it. We're interested in the medical applications, sure – but we also have humanitarian concerns too. If we hadn't sent a team, the tribe could just end up massacred like so many others, and then whatever secrets they held would go to the grave with them."

"But you don't really trust the Brazilian government either," Lee observed. "Professor Guzman certainly didn't."

Bakula shrugged. "Where there's money to be made, who can you really trust? That's another reason we wanted to be involved – we figured if a prestigious American university was involved, the Brazilians would be more likely to act honorably. Especially because the next stage would have been to contact the State Department about the discovery, if it was verified."

Lee nodded, and drank some more of his tea as he thought about the matter. He wasn't sure if contacting the US State Department was the best thing to do, but he supposed they might just be a little less corrupt than their Brazilian and Peruvian counterparts, so perhaps the involvement of the university research team *was* the lesser of several potential evils.

"If this tribe *does* exist," Lee said eventually, "and those anecdotal reports are true, then there might be another reason for their perceived immunity."

"That they *have* been contacted before?" Darrow asked. "And have built up their immunity in the normal way?"

Lee nodded his agreement, the logical side of his brain arguing that this was the most likely explanation for the whole thing.

"It's possible," Darrow continued, "and that's another reason we want to investigate, to find out if it *is* true. And then, there were other things said about the tribe too, that might indicate their immunology *is* something unique."

"Like what?"

"Like perfect teeth, above average height, great eyesight, little to no degenerative diseases, living to an unusually old age . . . the list goes on."

"A tribe of supermen," Lee commented, wondering if any of it could be true. "Or maybe aliens?"

"You don't believe it?" Bakula asked, slightly irritated.

Lee shrugged, coming to a conclusion about something. "Look," he said, "it doesn't matter if I think it's true or not. It's interesting, I'll give you that, but it's clouding the real issue. You sent in a team of researchers to find this tribe, and now they're missing. The rest is just window dressing."

"That's fair enough," Dunford said, before Bakula could respond again. "We're not asking you to believe in the exceptional properties of this tribe. We just want our team back."

"How many people are there on the team?" Lee asked, glad to be getting back to business.

"Six," Dunford said, extracting a manila envelope from his desk drawer and sliding it across to Lee. "All the details are in there, personnel files on all of them."

"There are others too," Darrow said. "Locals. We've got three guys from other tribes, ones who have only recently made contact with the outside world, they're acting as translators and guides. One of them is featured in Guzman's report as actually having had contact with the tribe in question before. And there's two more, professional trackers from Manaus."

"Protection?" Lee asked.

Dunford shook his head. "We considered contacting a private security firm," he said, "but we'd have been forced to explain ourselves, and we hardly wanted the word to spread. The tribespeople knew the score anyway, and the guys from Manaus were willing to go, without asking questions."

"Did they have weapons with them?"

"Our people didn't," Dunford said, "at least not so far as we were aware. Unless you include machetes and camp knives, of course. The trackers had rifles and handguns, and the tribesmen might have had a couple of short spears, and a bow and arrow, from the team's reports."

"You have information on these other people?"

"Not a great deal, but you'll be given whatever we have."

"Communications," Lee asked next, "how were they contacting you?"

"Satellite phone," Dunford answered.

"How many did the team have?"

"Two. The main, and a backup."

"Radios?"

"Everyone had a personal radio, as well as their own cellphones, for what they were worth in the middle of the Amazon."

"And you've not been able to raise them at all for the last week? Nothing whatsoever?"

Darrow shook her head. "Nothing," she said. "It's been terrible, we keep trying everything, but all the lines are dead, we're getting nothing."

"And just to confirm," Lee said, "it *is* everyone that has gone missing, yes? The trackers haven't been seen anywhere else, a tribesman hasn't turned up in another village?"

"As far as we know, it's the entire group," Dunford

said. "All gone."

Lee finished his tea and sat back in the chair, thinking. "What route did they use? Which bit of the rainforest are we actually looking at?"

Dunford entered some keystrokes onto the computer in front of him, and then turned the large flat-screen monitor around so that Lee could see it. It was a Google Earth image of South America, and Lee knew that Dunford had chosen the wide shot to give some perspective before zooming in. Sure enough, the image soon began to enlarge as Dunford zoomed in toward a region within the northwest section of the continent, a huge swath of the Amazon rainforest that straddled the border between southeast Peru and western Brazil.

"This is the area," Dunford said. "Thirty thousand square miles of mixed land use, with all sorts of conflicting laws and regulations. Sometimes it's referred to as one big 'reserve', but it's a lot more complex than that – you've got a communal reserve, indigenous lands, native communities, national parks, and 'reserves for indigenous peoples in isolation', which are prohibited to outsiders; although as we've mentioned before, that's widely ignored on the Peruvian side."

"So where did they go?"

"Flew into a small airfield in a place called Feijó," Dunford told him, pointing to the place on the screen, "then hired jeeps and went west along the main road – the 364, you can see it there – past Tarauacá, all the way until it meets the Juruá River, a tributary of the Amazon, right *here*." Dunford tapped the screen, and Lee saw where the highway was interrupted by the river. "Ferry boats are used to get vehicles across to the other side. Nothing fancy, mind, just a flat little boat that's about big enough to hold one car at a time. But they didn't cross the river, they met a boat there that they'd arranged, and it took them downriver."

"You know the people on the boat?" Lee asked.

"The actual police investigation did at least get that far," Bakula said. "They took our guys downriver, then returned – no funny business to report, if that's what you were thinking."

Lee nodded; that *was* what he'd been thinking. "How far downriver?" he asked.

Dunford tracked down the screen with his finger, and Lee watched as the river curved and spiraled to the southwest, before turning more directly southward, cutting through the thick vegetation of the surrounding rainforest. Dunford's finger stopped by the side of the river, just after a large horseshoe-shaped bend.

"Seringal Simpata," Dunford said. "Took them several days to navigate that damn river, and this is the last sign of known habitation in this particular area, it doesn't even really show up on here – I mean, it's literally just a few huts by the side of the river."

"And that's where they stopped?"

"Yeah," Darrow said. "The guides knew the area from there, and so they left the boats there and started making their way overland, to the west, into the *really* thick stuff."

"How many days ago was this?"

"That was a little less than three weeks ago," Darrow said. "Twenty days."

"So they were walking through there for nearly two weeks?" Lee asked. "What kind of supplies were they carrying?" From personal experience, he knew there was no way that anyone could carry two weeks' worth of provisions on their backs, while hiking through the sweltering rainforest.

"Supply drops," Bakula said, "provisions were carried in by airplane, then dropped over specific grid points every three days."

"And who arranged that?" Lee asked.

"Getting suspicious again, huh?" Bakula asked with a laugh. "It was Guzman who organized it, kept everything really sweet. Until we stopped hearing from them, that is."

"Where was the last message received from?"

"Last grid reference we have for them was right about *there*," Dunford said, pointing to a spot in the Serra do Divisor National Park that was less than ten kilometers from the Peruvian border. "Guzman's flights have been going over the area for days now, along with a couple of choppers from the police. But they've not seen anything at all, no sign of anyone. That rainforest is so thick though, it's probably a waste of time anyway – it's impossible to penetrate the canopy in that area, the only way to do it is to get eyes on the ground."

"Close to Peru," Lee commented. "Maybe they even crossed *into* Peru, at some point." He looked up at the three academics. "You think they might have stumbled across someone?" Hidden tribes, oil prospectors and illegal loggers were all contenders, but if the team had been murdered – and Lee had to grudgingly accept that this was a very real possibility – then drug gangs were the most likely culprits. The area was notorious for hidden drugs labs, and the rainforest was used as a secure route to smuggle cocaine from Peru and Columbia, into Brazil. If the team *had* stumbled into something they shouldn't have, then their prospects for survival weren't good at all. Snakes and jaguars, crocodiles and piranhas, and all the other assorted dangers of the Amazon, were concerns on an individual level, but were unlikely to have taken out an entire group of twelve people. Illness was likewise unlikely to have incapacitated them all. And why were all of the comms down?

Lee thought about the situation. Maybe the sat phone had broken – been dropped, or destroyed by water – and maybe the backup hadn't worked in the first place. No cellphone reception, and lousy personal radios that would struggle to get a signal very far. They wouldn't be able to log in their destination, and then wouldn't be able to get their resupplies. Hunger would result, even starvation eventually; but the real danger would have come from the lack of drinking water, which – in that heat – would have rendered them incapable within a single day. And yet the tribesmen would have known how to get water, and food if necessary. The trackers too, if they were any good. They'd have made a signal somehow too, used smoke to show Guzman where they were.

It was a mystery, but Lee's money was on some sort of human involvement. And if he was a betting man, he would have put his money on it being a drugs gang.

"I don't want to be too pessimistic about things," Lee said gravely, "but you need to understand the reality that – given the situation here – one of the best outcomes we can expect is for me to find their bodies, figure out what happened, and bring them home for burial."

They looked openly shocked at Lee's bluntness, but eventually, as one, they all nodded slightly. Of course they'd considered this; they were all highly educated people, how could they not? They must have known what the chances were of bringing this team back alive.

But if there was a chance – any at all – then damn it, Lee was going to be the man to do it.

"I'm gonna want to speak to this Professor Guzman guy," Lee said, focusing on the positives once again, trying to establish a workable plan of action.

Nervous glances were exchanged around the table once again, and Lee knew that another problem was about to come up.

"Professor Guzman," Dunford said eventually, "has . . . ah . . . gone off the radar too, let's say."

"Guzman's gone missing too?" Lee asked in surprise. "When?"

"Two days ago," Dunford confirmed. "It was the final push we needed to make us draft in some additional help." He smiled cagily at Lee. "Hence our call to you."

"Where was he last seen?" Lee asked, wondering how much worse the scenario could get.

"Feijó airport," Bakula answered. "Landed with the pilot after one of their search flights, called us from the airport, and that was the last we heard from him. According to the pilot, the guy went into the restroom, and didn't come out."

"The police chasing up on this?"

"Not seriously," Darrow said with obvious disgust.

"Okay," Lee said. "One more thing to contend with." *Damn*, he thought, *Alex had said this was something I could really get my teeth into, but what the hell am I getting involved in here?*

"Mr. Lee," Darrow said, getting his attention immediately with her sudden politeness. "This team, it's my team, I'm not sure if you understand, but I really need you to find them, I can't imagine never seeing them again, never even *hearing* from hem again."

"I *do* understand," Lee said, and it was true; bringing your people back was something that all military men and women understood perfectly. "You've heard that motto?" Lee asked. "'No Man Left Behind'?"

Darrow nodded. "Yes," she said.

"Well, Ms. Darrow, I live and breathe that motto. I base my life on it, my very existence."

Darrow's eyes moistened, and she bit her lip. "That's good to know," she said. "It is." She wiped her eyes, and looked at Lee. "I have a . . . personal stake in this too," she said.

"Oh?"

Darrow nodded. "Yes. One of the women on the team, Lisa Garfield, she and I . . . well, we have a relationship."

Tears *did* well up in her eyes now, and Lee's heart went out for her, imagining how terrible she must feel.

Darrow's hand went to her opposite wrist, and pulled off the watch that lay there. She put it on the table and pushed it across to him.

"Pick it up," she said, "look at the inscription."

Lee did as he was asked, turning the timepiece – which was surprisingly heavy-duty for a lady's wristwatch – over in his hands.

To Sylvia, the inscription read. *With love, always - LG*

Lee looked back up at her, saw the pleading in her eyes.

"Please take it with you," she said. "If you find her – when you find her – please give this to her, so she knows . . . she knows . . . that I'm thinking of her . . ."

Darrow started to sob in earnest then, and Bakula took her head and let her bury it in his shoulder.

Lee, seeing the depth of her feeling, took off his own watch and passed it across to Darrow, putting hers on his wrist in its place. The strap was on the last hole, but it fit.

"Ms. Darrow," he said. "I'll take my watch back when I return with your team. And you can rest assured," he continued, "that when you next see Lisa, she'll be wearing this."

Darrow nodded and blinked her appreciation, unable to speak, but the action spoke more than words could ever have done, and he resolved to do everything he could to successfully complete this seemingly impossible mission.

"Going back you your earlier point," Dunford said seriously, getting things back on track, "about the likelihood of . . . *survival*, as it were . . . well, we recognize that time is of the essence. Every day that goes by, without word from them, makes that survival less likely." Here, he glanced nervously at Darrow, hoping he wasn't upsetting her. "We *know* that. And we're also painfully aware of how long it took the team to get on-site in the first place – between flying, driving, boating and hiking, it was literally *weeks*. And I fear we just don't have this time. Do you think –"

Lee held up his hand, cutting Dunford off. "That's something you don't have to worry about," he assured them. "If we can sort out a plane from Feijó airport, I'll be onsite of their last known grid reference within an hour of take-off."

"You're going to parachute into the rainforest?" Dunford asked in open surprise.

"Well, we aren't called pararescue jumpers for nothing," Lee replied, smiling widely at the thought – despite the dangers, and the seeming impossibility – of what was to come.

Chapter Three

John Lee breathed in the hot, humid air as he looked around at the town of Feijó, from his position underneath the main gates. The warm, damp, fetid atmosphere reminded him of the jungles of northern Thailand, and his time in the monastery there.

Involuntarily, he thought momentarily about the reason he escaped into his self-imposed exile, saw the last few seconds of his wife's and daughter's lives flash before him; then he remembered Phoenix, ensconced in the hotel with Marcus Hartman, and the spell was broken.

Why the hell had he agreed to bring her? It wasn't safe here, his gut told him. And yet she was the team's technical specialist, and monitoring Lee's mission from nearby – relatively, at least – made sense, on a practical level. Mabuni had provided him with certain toys that he actually *might* make use of for this job, and Phoenix would act as his eyes and ears as she remotely monitored the information he sent back. Finding the team was still going to be one hell of a task, but he welcomed all the help he could get. And yet . . .

"She shouldn't be here," Lee muttered to himself, as he walked down the dirty, mud road that ran through the center of town, scanning a crowd that consisted of a handful of backpacker-tourists and plenty of locals, dressed in the ubiquitous shorts and sandals, whatever their age. Nearby, a stream of old cars and puttering scooters ran past them in both directions, diesel fumes mixing with the hot air, making him choke.

Trying to forget about Phoenix, Lee reminded himself of the directions to the local police station, where he'd arranged to meet Emmanuel Rodrigues, the deputy commander.

After his meeting in Chicago, Lee had flown back to Miami, where he'd met Phoenix at the airport for the onward flight to Manaus, an international airport that acted as the gateway to the Amazon. Hartman had also been there, to arrange for secure transportation of Lee's weapons and equipment, which Mabuni had stressed *were* to be used, this time.

From Manaus, Hartman had arranged a charter flight to Feijó, and the three of them had arrived just two hours ago. They'd taken a taxi with their secure luggage to the Hotel Joafran – the same place that the Chicago team had stayed the month before – and Lee had left the other two there, to set up their headquarters, while he had quickly headed out onto the streets of the town. Lee knew that time was of the essence, and was keen to get things moving.

Back at the airport – which wasn't much more than an airstrip in the middle of the jungle, really – Lee had seen a couple of aircraft that belonged to Rio Branco Aerotaxi, alongside a handful of other small planes that the guard on duty said were privately owned. Further enquiries showed that one of them belonged to Eduardo Silva, the pilot who had been flying Guzman around for the past few weeks – first to drop off supplies, and then to search for the missing team.

Silva wasn't at the airport, and didn't seem to have a cellphone, or any other way of contacting him. But the guard had mentioned that if he was likely to be anywhere, it would be at Bar Uniao, where he'd been seen the past couple of days, drinking himself into oblivion.

He was someone else that Lee would be speaking to that day, if he could be found; and Lee wholeheartedly wished he could be, as Silva was obviously perfectly placed to act as the pilot for this mission, seeing as how he was the only person around familiar with the route taken by the missing group.

He wandered the streets of Feijó for a good thirty minutes while trying to spot a tail, wondering all the while about Guzman and the pilot. He saw a couple of people who might have been watching him, but they appeared to be locals, and it might just have been that they didn't see that many tourists in town, and were just staring out of natural curiosity. Either way, by the time he'd turned onto Avenue Plácido de Castro – the street where the police station was located – they had gone on their way. Lee had committed their faces to memory though, just in case they appeared anywhere else. Seeing a guy once was one thing, but if the same person appeared twice, then alarm bells should always start ringing.

He looked down the street once again as he crossed the road, double-checking for those locals. If Guzman had been murdered – as Lee suspected – then it *was* possible that someone was watching him right now, tracking his arrival and subsequent movements through Feijó. Who it might be though, Lee couldn't say. Members of a drug gang, private security hired by loggers or oil companies, even agents from intelligence agencies, the list of people who might be involved was long and disturbing. It might even be a rival university, Lee figured, although Dunford and the others had thought the idea crazy. They firmly believed that such institutions were bastions of morality. Lee, for his part, wasn't so sure.

Lee was glad that Hartman was in the hotel with Phoenix. He'd been a logistics specialist in the army, but the man knew his way around a rifle. He'd seen action in both Afghanistan and Iraq, and was a real pro. In fact, although Lee himself eschewed lethal weapons, Hartman hade made sure to pack a Colt M4A1 assault carbine, along with a few of Mabuni's special "home defense" devices. As per Lee's requirements, the devices were all non-lethal, but he knew Hartman would use the rifle if he had to, and Lee wasn't about to tell him he couldn't. If it was a life or death situation, the man had the right to defend himself – and Phoenix – in the best way possible. Lee was sure that the hotel room was about as secure as it could be, and it put his mind at rest as he spotted the police station across the road.

The building was larger than Lee had expected; given the remoteness of the location, he'd thought the station might be little more than a guard shack. But then again, he supposed, the town *was* home to over thirty thousand people. It was a one-story white-painted block with a sloping roof and an archway in the center with a ramp that led inside. There was a 4x4 cop car outside, and a carport full of motorbikes. Two cops, handguns on hips, stood outside, smoking and chatting.

Lee passed the two cops outside, walked up the wooden ramp, and turned left toward what looked like the main office, wondering – perhaps too late – if the police might be involved in this too.

"Mr. Lee," Deputy Commander Rodrigues said warmly, shaking hands with Lee before they took their seats opposite each other, a cluttered, workmanlike desk between them. The office was small and incredibly hot, even with the window open and the ceiling fan working overtime. Lee gazed out of the window, saw that it looked out onto Avenue Plácido de Castro, could see the strong sun reflecting off the hood of the 4x4.

Rodrigues shifted some of the paperwork to one side, before propping his elbows on the table and steepling his hands under his chin. "So, you are here about Professor Guzman, yes?"

"Yes," Lee said. "Professor Guzman, and the US team that he was searching for."

"Ah yes," Rodrigues said, as if he'd already forgotten all about them, "the Americans. They still haven't turned up, as I understand it."

"I thought you were investigating it?"

"Mr. Lee," the cop said, hands gesturing to the air around him, "do you see our resources here? That team was last seen hundreds of kilometers away, in a rainforest that – at that location – is almost, how do you say . . . impenetration?"

"Impenetrable," Lee said.

Rodrigues raised his hands and shoulders, as if that explained everything. "Impenetrable. Yes. I mean, what do you think we can do, really? Send everyone out into the forest to look for them?" He laughed, and shook his head. "We would never find them anyway."

Lee tried not to show his anger over the cop's attitude. Things were different out here, he knew, and he had to remind himself of that; and if he upset the deputy commander of the local police department, he might well end up in a jail cell rather than heading out on his rescue mission.

"And Professor Guzman?" Lee asked.

Rodrigues pulled out a cigar before he answered, offering Lee one from the box. Lee shook his head, the cop shrugged and put a match to the end, filling the room with the acrid odors of the cheap cigar.

Rodrigues puffed away on it happily for several moments, before answering Lee's question. "We suspect that Professor Guzman has run away with a local girl," he said at last, waving away some of the smoke.

Lee could barely believe what he was hearing. "You think what?"

"We think this is connected to a romance the honorable professor was having with . . . ah . . ." – he broke off to leaf through one of the papers on his desk – ". . . a girl named Alessandra Torres. Yes," he confirmed, jabbing his finger at the report, "Torres. A barmaid from town, suspected of other, let us say, more intimate work too, yes? Well, we have received numerous eyewitness accounts that Guzman was seen in the company of this woman for several days before he went missing, perhaps a week or more. You know, he'd go out in the plane, fly around all day, then meet this woman at night." He puffed on the cigar a bit more, and held Lee's gaze. "You know he was married, yes?"

Lee nodded. He did know, although he didn't see how it mattered in this particular case. If Guzman had been involved with a woman down here, then it was morally questionable perhaps, but that didn't mean she was involved in his disappearance, didn't mean he'd run away with her.

"You've got evidence that he was with this woman," Lee pointed out, "but do you have anything concrete to indicate that he definitely left town with her?"

"We checked his hotel room, no sign of – how do you call it? – foul play, yes? And his luggage was gone, room paid for."

"In person?"

"What?"

"I mean, did he pay the bill himself, did anyone see him pay the bill?"

Rodrigues shrugged again. "Nobody remembers."

"So, an open and shut case, right?" Lee asked with a raised eyebrow.

Rodrigues grinned broadly, showing all of his yellow, stained teeth at the same time. "I am glad you understand, my friend. An open and shut case, that is right." He waved more of the smoke away, although the office was so small, it had nowhere to go. "He will probably turn up somewhere in a day or two, you know? Manaus maybe, perhaps Rio, who knows?"

"Well," Lee said, realizing he was not going to get anywhere further with Rodrigues, "thank you for your time. An efficient little operation you've got here."

Rodrigues' eyes narrowed, and Lee wondered if he'd recognized the sarcasm in his tone. But then the friendliness – and the smile – were back in full force as he stood and held out his hand in farewell, banging the desk with his leg as he pushed himself out of his chair, knocking over some more of the papers.

Lee took it, and as he shook the hand, his eyes wandered down to the desk, taking in the newly scattered paperwork that lay across it.

His subconscious brain picked it up before he properly recognized what he was seeing but – when he did – he froze, eyes locked onto it.

It was a black-and-white crime-scene photograph,

still half-hidden under a pile of other documents; but it was enough for Lee to recognize the face of Professor Hector Guzman, from the file provided by Dunford. Half of the skull had been shattered by what could only have been a gunshot, the ground around his head a halo of blood, his eyes black and almost forced from their sockets by the eight-ball hemorrhage.

The deputy commander had been lying; the reasons didn't matter, for the time being at least, but the fact that the cop had sat there and sold Lee a line about Guzman running off with a woman while he had photographs of the dead man on his desk, meant that things were about to go downhill very quickly.

Rodrigues noticed the sudden tension in Lee's body, his eyes flicking down to his desk, and Lee knew the man understood what Lee had seen.

Within an instant, the cop tried to jerk Lee forward by his hand, throwing a short punch toward his head as he did so. Lee slipped to the side, slamming his open palm into the cop's chest, breaking the handgrip and sending him sprawling back into his chair.

Rodrigues was fast though, drawing his handgun even as he fell backwards. By the time he hit the chair, it was already up and aimed in Lee's direction. With nowhere to run in the small office, but with Rodrigues out of reach of his arms, Lee felt himself already pivoting on the ball of one foot, the other leg whipping around and over the desk in a spinning kick that hit the cop on the wrist, smashing the arm wide.

Rodrigues squeezed the trigger even as the rotator

cuff of his shoulder was blown apart completely, and even though the round buried itself in the wall and missed Lee entirely, the sound of the shot was deafening in the tiny room and he knew it would bring the other cops running.

Rodrigues started to yell, as if the sound of the shot wasn't enough, and Lee leaped across the desk and took the cop out with a jumping front kick to the face that blasted Rodrigues backward, his head whiplashing against the rear wall.

Lee turned and raced to the office door, pulling it open before slamming it shut again when he heard boots racing down the corridor, accompanied by the sound of men shouting loudly in Portuguese.

Lee ran past the desk, the unconscious body of Rodrigues still slumped behind it, and as he went, he picked up the chair he'd been sitting in just moments before.

He was already swinging it as he reached the window, smashing it apart when it made impact, shards flying into the street outside, Lee following them as he jumped through the open frame, body narrowly missing the jagged edges that remained.

He hit the concrete outside and rolled, coming up to his feet in one fluid motion. It was no harder – indeed, it was actually easier – than many of the stunts he'd had to perform with the movie studio in Hong Kong back in his younger days, but at least back then, he didn't have to worry about people trying to shoot him with real guns. Not on the set, anyway.

This time, as he came up into a crouch, he scanned the area and immediately saw the two cops who'd been chatting and smoking earlier. Alerted by the gunfire, and then the broken window, they both had their weapons out, and were tracking them toward Lee.

Lee double-stepped across the hot asphalt and kicked the first man in the gut, doubling him over and making him drop the gun; and at the same time, his hand went to his belt and took it off in one smooth action, letting it whip out toward the second man, the buckle making contact with the guy's forearm. The cop yelled in pain and dropped the weapon, and Lee whipped the belt back into the first cop's face, the buckle catching him above the eye and stunning him, knocking him to the ground. A moment later and the belt was whistling through the air again, striking the second cop in the groin, dropping him to the ground with his friend, accompanied by a high-pitched squeal of pain.

Lee's eyes quickly took in the scene, heard doors opening through the archway, knew he would see armed men racing toward him moments later, and he was moving again quickly, sprinting for the carport and the motorbikes.

His heart racing, he selected the first bike he saw, swinging his leg over it even as he went to work on the ignition, all too aware that within seconds, cops with pistols, shotguns and maybe even assault rifles would be turning into the garage. But then the engine caught, and he accelerated out of the car port, turning the bike toward the station's archway rather than away from it, knowing his only chance of escape was to attack whoever was there; if he tried to race away, he'd almost certainly get a bullet in the back just instants later.

He saw the men as he turned the corner, was gratified to see the surprise on their faces as they realized the bike was heading right for them. There were four cops, three with semi-auto pistols, one with a pump action shotgun, and two of them managed to dive out of the way as Lee drove right at them. The other two, slightly out of the direct path, started to raise their guns, but Lee kicked one in the balls on his way past, then took out the other with the belt, which he whipped into the guy's temple.

Lee screeched around in a tight arc, and started to move in the opposite direction, targeting the two remaining men, who'd managed to jump clear on the first run. They were to either side of the bike, their backs to Lee but turning toward him, and Lee put his weight forward onto the handlebars, balancing himself as he kicked out with both legs simultaneously, smashing his boots into the men's faces as they turned.

A fraction of a second later and he was sat back on the bike, accelerating away down Plácido de Castro. He heard shots fired a few seconds later, but knew it was too little, too late; he was away now, and the chances of them getting a hit at this distance were slim. But still he hunkered down over the bars, keeping his head low between his shoulders, only relaxing slightly when he made a left turn onto President Kennedy, leaving the cops behind.

He knew they would be on his tail soon though, once they'd got themselves together, and he pulled out his cellphone as he raced the bike down the narrow streets and alleyways of Feijó, dialing Phoenix's secure cellphone.

"It's me," he breathed as the call was answered. "Stop whatever it is you're doing, get everything together, and meet me at the airport, as quickly as you can."

"What happened?" came the reply, voice tight with worry.

"It doesn't matter. Just get there with Marcus, I'll meet you there."

"Where are you now?"

"On my way to get us a pilot," he replied, hoping desperately that Eduardo Silva would be at Bar Uniao.

Because if he wasn't, Lee didn't know what the hell he was going to do.

Chapter Four

Lee pulled up outside the bar, hearing the sound of sirens in the distance. If Rodrigues had woken up by now, then he'd have certainly sent his troops straight to the Hotel Joafran. Lee was in no doubt that the deputy commander would know exactly where they were staying, which was one of the reasons why Lee had been so concerned that Phoenix and Marcus move as quickly as possible. Feijó as a base of operations was out of the picture now, and they were going to have to get up in the air with him if they wanted to escape arrest – for he would surely be brought in for questioning, at the very least.

He burst through into the bar – which was just a one-story shack on a narrow dirt road – and his eyes took in the scene in seconds. It was small, a long bar running the length of one wall and about a dozen tables scattered over the tiled floor. There were two older guys at a table at one end, a young couple that looked like tourists a little closer, and three or four regulars propping up the bar itself. Behind the bar, wiping off glasses, was a guy in his sixties that looked like he'd worked there his entire life.

He strode over to the guys at the bar, who'd all turned to observe the new customer, and stared down the line. "Eduardo Silva," Lee announced, hoping beyond hope that the pilot would be there.

Nobody moved, but Lee observed a tiny flicker of the eyes from one of the customers, and the barman, toward the guy sitting on the end stool. Late forties, with a short crewcut and a weather-beaten face like old leather, the guy had a paunch to his belly that hung slightly over the belt of his cargo shorts. There wasn't even a flicker of response at the mention of the name Eduardo Silva, but Lee knew it was him from the body language of the others. Or at least, *hoped* it would be him.

With everyone in the bar staring straight at him, Lee marched around to the far end and put his hand on the shoulder of the man he believed was Silva.

"Eduardo Silva," he whispered to him. "You need to come with me. Right now."

"*Eu não entendo*," the man said gruffly, shrugging off Lee's hand.

Lee reached in even closer, his mouth close to the man's ear, and used what little Portuguese he knew. "*Ouço*," he said, drawing the man's attention to the sounds of sirens on the streets of Feijó. "*Polícia. Para voce.*" He tapped the man on the shoulder again to emphasize the point.

Listen. Police. For you.

That got the man's attention, Lee saw, the eyes instantly worried; and if he *was* Silva, then why wouldn't he be worried? His last customer had been brutally murdered, and the police certainly seemed to be involved in it somehow.

"Hector Guzman?" Lee asked sadly, before placing a hand on his own chest. "*Amigos.*" He pointed to door, noise of sirens somewhere beyond. "*Vamos.*"

Let's go.

Finally, the man nodded his head, and asked the barman for the bill, standing from the stool as he reached into his pocket for his wallet.

Come on, dammit, let's go already . . .

And then Lee felt the atmosphere in the room change, saw that Silva – if that's who he was – was actually reaching for a gun instead of a wallet, was pulling it on Lee; and as Lee's hand jammed the guy's arm at the elbow, stopping the draw, the man next to them was trying to smash Lee's head open with a bottle of whisky.

Lee got his elbow up in an instant, slamming the bony tip into the inside of the man's forearm, causing him to drop the bottle onto the floor, where it shattered; and at the sound, everyone started to move at the same time, like runners bursting off the starting blocks.

Lee saw the barman reaching low, knew he was going for a shotgun or similar weapon under the bar, and he whipped a high roundhouse kick over the bar top, instep of his foot slamming into the guy's head. As the barman dropped unconscious behind the bar, Lee grabbed the gun out of Silva's hand and pistol-whipped the man who'd been holding the bottle at the same time as banging Silva's head off the bar top.

As both men slid off their stools and onto the floor, Lee saw the older guys standing up from their table, both pulling what looked like WWII-era Colt .45s from somewhere. Lee sighed internally – what the hell kind of place was this? But he was already moving, throwing first Silva's gun, and then his own barstool, at the two men. The gun hit the guy on the left square in the face, and the second guy barely managed to get his arms up in time to protect himself; but both of their weapons were off-target, at least for now, and Lee swept to the side as he felt the blow come from behind, turning to confront the other two men at the bar.

The first held a Bowie knife that barely missed carving a canyon out of Lee's chest, and behind him was the second, with a .38 snub-nose revolver. The first guy had already missed with the knife, and would need a moment to recover, and so Lee attacked the man with the gun, launching an inner-crescent kick that caught the guy on the inside of the wrist and sent the weapon wide, the bullet shattering the mirrors behind the bar. With the same leg, Lee pushed the man away with a side kick before turning to the guy with the knife, who was coming back for a second pass. Lee struck him in the side of the neck with the callused edge of one hand as he blocked the incoming knife arm with the other, and Lee turned again before he'd even seen the man drop, knowing that unconsciousness was inevitable. He picked up two more barstools as he turned, throwing them back towards the old guys at the end of the bar. They covered up again as the stools sailed toward them, and Lee turned once again, to see the guy with the revolver moving the weapon back in his direction. Assessing the distance quickly, Lee hooked his foot under the bottom of another bar stool before lifting his leg hard, sending it sailing toward the gunman, who reflexively dropped the revolver and caught the piece of furniture before it hit him in the face. Lee shot in, grabbed the legs that were facing him and jerked the stool forward, the seat of the stool smashing into the guy's face anyway. And then he pulled the stool away and fired a full-power front kick into the man's chest that sent him flying backwards out of the front door, into the street beyond.

Lee looked around quickly, saw that five men were unconscious, with the two older guys sprawled under the barstools at the end of the room. The only people uninjured, except for Lee himself, were the two young tourists, who were still sitting in their chairs, staring at him open-mouthed.

Before they could say anything, Lee grabbed Silva off the floor, saw he was still out of it, and hauled him up over his shoulders in a fireman's carry before racing for the door.

Moments later, he was back out into the bright daylight, nearly blinding after the relative darkness of the bar, but he found the bike quickly, the body of the man he'd kicked through the doors lying right next to it, and he laid Silva out on top of the bike before jumping on himself and gunning the engine.

Amazingly, there were still no cops on the street, and Lee accelerated away, turning at the sound of the bar doors opening again behind him. It was the old guys from the far end, waving their ancient Colt .45s around again.

But he knew there was no chance they'd hit him on the bike, and he grinned, wishing he had a couple more bar stools to throw at them.

Chapter Five

"Where the hell are they?" Phoenix asked Hartman, as she paced around the airstrip.

"Damned if I know," the big guy answered. "He still not answering the cell?"

"No," said Phoenix, looking down at the screen once more to see if he'd called back. But still, there was nothing, and the police channel was lighting up like a Christmas tree. Phoenix was on the police frequencies, scanning them through a real-time translation program that put everything directly into English for them as they listened. The Feijó PD was after an "armed and dangerous" criminal, of "Oriental appearance", who had attacked the police station, and they seemed determined to get their man.

Cops had also been sent their way, to the Hotel Joafran, but Phoenix and Hartman had been long gone by the time the hotel had been raided, packing up and leaving as soon as Lee had placed the call. They'd arrived at the airport in record time, and Hartman had already started sweettalking the owner of the Aerotaxi firm into getting them out of there, if Lee didn't turn up with a pilot. If push came to shove, Hartman was willing to steal a plane to get out of there. Lee would be able to fly it; although he was no expert, he knew enough to get them up and – hopefully – to land the thing again. If they went down that route though, it would mean rethinking the entire plan, because Lee couldn't parachute out of the plane he was piloting. Well, not if he wanted Phoenix and Hartman to live, anyway.

No, Phoenix knew that the ideal solution was for Lee to turn up with Silva before the police did, and for them all to fly out of there. Once in the air, they could find out what Silva knew, and he could then take them to the right area, where Lee could parachute out with his equipment. Silva could then carry on to another destination, where they could set up a secondary headquarters. Phoenix had already scoped out a couple of potential sites in other locations, and had backup plans already in place. Tarauaca was the closest, but potentially within easy reach of the cops if they decided to continue the pursuit. Cruzeiro do Sul was further afield, and perhaps the safer bet.

"What was that?" Hartman asked, turning to the radios. "What did they say?"

They both stopped and listened, aghast.

The cops had found him.

Lee saw the bikes turning into the residential street

ahead of him. There were two of them, and they were already on their radios, telling the others.

The trouble – or one of them, anyway – was that he didn't know how many cops Feijó had available. Was it six? Or sixty? Lee had no idea, and the lack of knowledge made him nervous.

But he had more immediate things to deal with here, and as the cops approached, he turned his bike sharply to the right, heading toward the open front door of a small house. The bike bumped up the two entry steps, then sped inside the house, and Lee negotiated a corner around a beaten-up old sofa and into the kitchen, past an old woman kneading dough at the counter, mouth open in shock.

"*Desculpa!*" he yelled over the noise of the engine, frighteningly loud in such a confined space, as he bumped open the door to the rear yard and left the woman behind.

He bounced out into a small yard, and burst through a small gate into the yard of another house that backed onto the first. He heard the bark of a dog, and turned to see a huge Rottweiler heading his way, a man reclining on a sun-lounger leaping up and yelling as he accelerated to the side of the house and smashed through the wooden gate, the dog hot on their trail.

The bike blasted out onto another road, this one lined with a few local shops as well as houses, and a couple of small cafes. The road was wider, with a bit of traffic, and Lee gunned the engine and pushed the little bike harder, hoping to make some distance while losing himself in the other vehicles.

He wondered if Rodrigues would figure that he was making a run for the airport, and decided it was likely. But would he divert resources away from the main chase? Again, it was down to how many people he had working for him.

He heard sirens again, and turned to see the 4x4 heading into the street behind him, two more motorcycle outriders with it. He'd only had a glance – he couldn't afford to take his eyes off the road for too long, while weaving in and out of traffic – but he was pretty sure that Rodrigues was the passenger seat of the 4x4.

The traffic started to snarl up a bit further ahead, and – knowing he had no time to lose – Lee mounted the sidewalk, people scattering as he raced along, missing them by inches.

He risked a glance behind and saw the 4x4 was getting held up, while the bikes followed his lead, darting onto the sidewalk after him.

He headed toward a grocery, outdoor baskets full of fruits and vegetables, brightly colored in the midday sun. Customers leaped out of the way as they saw him approaching, and he slowed down, knowing the two bikes would be closing in but wanting to take a risk in order to get rid of them.

He reached the stands of fruit and kicked out at the bases as he went past, putting his boot through the wooden legs that held them. They collapsed as he moved past, hundreds of items falling and rolling onto the sidewalk.

He looked over his shoulder to see the first cop get there, the fruit running under the tires, some of it being crushed to juice, while more of it unbalanced the bike and caused it to topple sideways, until the rider was collapsed to the floor; and then his partner, seeing the danger, steered off into the street, only to be sideswiped by a passing taxi and knocked off his bike completely.

Lee breathed out. He could see the town gates ahead, and knew it was only a short distance then to the airport, maybe four kilometers at the most.

He just had to hope that Silva would be awake when they got there.

"He's coming!" screamed Phoenix excitedly. Lee had called her already to tell them to get the equipment onto Silva's airplane – either the pilot would fly them out of there, or he'd do it himself, and work out the rest of the plan from there – but now she could see him, and that made it real.

But there was still a body – possibly unconscious – draped over his bike and, following closely behind, what appeared to be a convoy of a dozen police vehicles, including three cruisers, a 4x4, and a whole bunch of motorbikes. Lee was in the lead – just – and the whole convoy was spraying up so much dust into the atmosphere as they raced toward the airport, it must have been almost impossible to see anything at all for the people at the rear.

Hartman raced toward the gate, ignoring the

terrified cries of the airport staff, and he readied himself with the rifle. Phoenix knew he wasn't going to go full-crazy and open fire on a whole police department, but he might take a few well-aimed shots at the tires.

"Come on!" she heard him shout to Lee, who was close now, so close, the nearest vehicles just a hundred yards behind, bullets firing everywhere, like a fourth of July fireworks parade.

"Get ready to close the gate!" Lee yelled at Hartman, who nodded and readied himself.

Lee was just fifty yards away now, forty, thirty, twenty, and now some of the shots were peppering the metal fence line, ricocheting everywhere; and then Lee was through into the airport compound, shouting "Now!" at Hartman, who was already moving, pushing the metal gates closed and firing a few warning shots toward the oncoming police vehicles before turning and racing after Lee.

Lee screeched to a stop by the airplane, hauling Silva off the bike and to his feet, slapping him in the face to try and get some life back into him.

"Silva," Lee said. "I know you understand English, so listen to me. If you don't get us out of here, we're *dead*, you got that? All of us."

Silva's eyes opened wider, then narrowed, then went wide again. "Who are you?" he asked in English, before looking over Lee's shoulder and seeing the invading hordes stopped outside the gate, lining up to try and fire through the fence line. "Woah," he said, coming almost to attention, adrenaline bringing all the life back into him now, "it doesn't matter. Come on, let's get the hell out of here, you can tell me when we're in the sky." He had already broken out of Lee's grip, and was heading for the cockpit.

"Hey," Hartman called after him, "you sober enough to fly?"

"Hey, *you*," Silva fired back as he climbed aboard. "I always fly better when I'm drunk. Now, you coming, or what?"

Nobody had to be asked twice, and they were all onboard seconds later; and a few seconds after that, the engines were firing up, and the plane was moving.

"So much for safety checks," muttered Hartman as he guarded the door with the M4, watching as the cops worked to break down the fence, shouting orders for the airport officials to stop them.

But there was no stopping them now, as Silva got the plane taxiing toward the runway in record time, getting there just as the gates broke open and the Feijó police department invaded the airfield, racing toward them.

At the front of the plane, Silva breathed deep, hit the throttle and – as the cruisers and bikes and 4x4 chased them down the runway, gunfire raging behind them – he accelerated hard toward the horizon until eventually, finally, mercifully, the little plane broke gravity and lifted off the airfield, into the azure blue skies above, and then they were away . . .

To freedom.

CHAPTER SIX

Lee looked down at the vast emerald expanse of pristine rainforest that lay below them, spread out like a magnificent, shimmering carpet of verdant, primal beauty, and his heart soared.

He had been half-expecting Rodrigues to order a plane up into the air after them, but – although there was a lot of impotent screaming and shouting across the police band – nobody else took off from the airfield to catch them. In fact, it appeared they were in the clear – for now, at least. Lee had already established that the Piper Seneca III twin-engine light aircraft they were in was fully fueled, and gave them a range of over seven hundred nautical miles, more than enough to get wherever they wanted to go.

It was plush inside despite its three decades of use, and they'd even found space for their equipment. Some of it was loaded into the gull-winged cargo area, while they kept other items – such as Lee's parachute, and the equipment he hoped to be jumping with – in the cabin with them.

The equipment was stashed into a large backpack, which Lee would carry through the forest with him. There were rations and bottled water, as well as tabs to treat any other water he found when that ran out, a first aid kit, hi-tech cameras and recording equipment, a sat-phone and a military-grade radio, a hardened GPS tracker, a hardened laptop, some of Mabuni's special weapons, and a special drone aircraft which could give him a real-time view from above, if he got lost or needed some visual information. The signals would also be sent back to Phoenix, who would be monitoring it all from her new HQ.

And, of course, there was another set of night vision goggles, which he'd promised Mabuni he would *definitely* wear this time.

The accommodation in the cabin was split into two rows of two leather armchairs, set facing each other, with luggage space behind the rear row and the front row backing on to the two seats up front, for a pilot and co-pilot. Lee was sitting in the co-pilot's seat, grilling the man next to him, who -true to his word – was doing a good job of flying the plane while drunk.

"So, you don't think it was the cops who killed Guzman?" Lee asked, turning his attention away from the forest and back to the pilot.

"No," Silva said, in accented English not helped by a slur that came from the drink, "it was *not* the cops, I am sure of it. But they know who killed him, certain people – like your friend, Deputy Commander

Rodrigues down there – have been paid off, that is for sure. That's why I've been at that bar, not drinking my life away man, no, no, no – well maybe a little – but that's not the reason, it's because I know people there, I was protected there, you know? Although," he said as he touched his broken nose, courtesy of having his head smashed off the bar by Lee, "not as protected as I thought, eh?"

"Well, at least it was the good guys who found you, right?"

Silva touched his face again. "Hmmm. Maybe," was all he allowed.

"So, if not the police, then who?"

"Ah, well that is the question, isn't it? I suppose the answer is, if I knew, I wouldn't be alive, don't you agree?"

Lee thought about it, and decided the man was right. "But you must have some idea of what happened though," he said, trying to prize *some* information out of him, at least.

The pilot shrugged helplessly. "What can I say? Obviously, someone who wanted to keep him quiet. Or else, someone who wanted to know what he knew."

"What *did* he know?"

Silva shrugged again. "The reason those crazy American assholes went into the forest in the first place."

"Do *you* know the reason?"

"Again," Silva said, "if I did, do you think I'd still be alive? No, I'm just the tour guide, I do not know a thing except how to fly this plane. But Guzman knew, and I suppose somebody *knew* he knew." Silva shrugged once more. "Or maybe not."

"You see anyone strange about town?" Lee asked. "Around the time of the murder?"

"There are always some strange people in Feijó, my friend, hey?" At this, the man started to roar with laughter; Lee just waited for it to subside. "Yes, always strange people. But lately, yes. Americans."

"Americans?" Lee asked, his interest piqued. "Are you sure?"

"Of course I am sure, I make my living flying American tourists around. Sometimes European, sometimes Chinese or Russian, but mainly American. So yes, I am sure."

"Who were they?"

"I don't know."

"What were they doing?"

"I don't know, but the day after Guzman went missing, so had they – although I think one of my competitors at the airfield might have taken them somewhere, you know?"

"Out over the rainforest?"

"Maybe," Silva allowed. "He didn't want to talk about it, either been paid too much, or was too scared. Anyway, I had a bad feeling since Guzman went missing, so I spent most of my time in that bar you found me in, I didn't hear much else about it. But yes, I think they were taken into the forest."

"How many of them?" Lee asked, thinking that

drawing information out of Silva was like getting blood from a stone. A minute ago, he had no idea who could have killed Guzman. Now, it seemed like he had might have some real answers.

"I am not sure, but in town, I noticed maybe four or five, I do not know if there were more."

"You sure they weren't tourists?" Lee asked.

"They were not tourists, my friend. They pretended to be perhaps, but they were not. Again, after so many years, I have a . . . *nose* for these sorts of things, yes?"

"What did they look like?"

"Tough," was all Silva offered.

Lee's heart was racing, despite himself. Who were they, and what were they doing here? Was it another team, after the same thing as the Chicago academics? Was it private contractors, hired by some company with a vested interest? Or was it an intelligence agency, maybe the CIA itself?

It could also have something to do with drugs, Lee knew; perhaps some assistance in tackling the cartels' drug routes, from SOF "advisors"?

And yet the timing was too much of a coincidence, and he knew that although such coincidences *did* happen, they were rare things indeed, and his gut told him that everything was connected.

"Phoenix," he said, turning to the rear of the plane. "Did you hear that?"

"Already on it," she said, tapping away at her secure laptop. "I'll try and access airport records, pull passport data and see if I can learn anything."

She was good, Lee had to admit, and her brilliance was one of the things that attracted him to her, although he rarely told her. He didn't tell her this time either, instead turning back to look out of the cockpit window, deep in thought as the green carpet rushed by below them at one hundred and forty miles per hour. Dunford had been right, there was no way you could see anything on the ground through that canopy, and he marveled at the sheer scale of the Amazon. Deforestation might have been happening at an alarming rate, but for Lee, all he could see – in front, to the left, to the right – was rainforest, everywhere, covering every inch of earth around them.

From this vantage point, he could well imagine the impossibility of knowing everything there was to know about this wilderness, so hidden from the view of the outside world. How many unknown tribes – perhaps entire civilizations – had lived and died under the protection of its vast canopy? It covered 3.4 million miles, which was more than half the size of the United States. What, Lee wondered, if half of the United States was covered by such a canopy? It was nearly unthinkable. What secrets would that canopy cover? And what secrets lay beneath them now?

Could there be a tribe down there somewhere, immune to illnesses of every kind? And if there were, then what were the ramifications of such a find? He could see why the university was so keen to send a team here, despite the risks – such a discovery could revolutionize medicine, in ways unprecedented.

He checked the heavy watch he'd been given by Sylvia Darrow – and which he'd pledged to pass over to a woman named Lisa Garfield – then the map that lay in front of him, then the cockpit's GPS locator, and looked at Silva. "How long?" he asked.

"We'll be over your destination in about . . . twenty minutes," Silva replied. "You sure you want to do this?"

"It's my job," Lee told him as he started to climb over his seat to the rear, reaching for the parachute. "This is what I do."

PART TWO

Chapter One

The wind whipped at Lee's body as he fell through the sky, battered and buffeted as the incredible emerald landscape raced upward to meet him.

He'd just left the aircraft, having taken a visual of the exact spot he wanted to land in before jumping; he could still hear the plane above him, carrying on toward Cruzeiro do Sul, where Phoenix and Marcus would set up her secondary headquarters.

The jump wasn't too hard, on a technical level; he'd been parachuting for fun since he was a teenager, and had received the best tactical jump training that the US military had to offer – HALO, HAHO, low-level jumps, night insertions, he'd done them all, and had gone onto make many operational jumps too. But it was the landing that made things dangerous – if he made any sort of mistake when he entered the canopy, broken legs would be the best he could hope for. A rope-insertion might have been preferable into a forest environment, but that required a helicopter, which they didn't have here.

The aim was to pull the chute almost immediately, once clear of the plane, and then drift comfortably to his chosen position while releasing the heavy equipment pack that he carried, so that it hung beneath him, secured by a line; it would enter the canopy first, breaking a way through for him, and then he would follow, legs stiff and toes pointed as he penetrated the tree tops in the area with the thinnest covering he could identify.

He knew he had space now, and pulled the chute, felt the reassuring pull as it was released from the pack on his back, the wind entering the silk chute and arresting his fall violently.

But not violently enough, he realized, and he looked up quickly, saw that the main canopy was tangled in the lines, was failing to fill properly with air, the silk billowing but collapsing as it began to wrap around itself, and Lee felt the lurch in his stomach as he continued to fall.

His hands worked fast, born of years of practice, and he quickly went for the lines, trying to untangle them as he fell through the sky toward the treetops below, still coming up fast; too fast, he realized, knowing if he left it too late, he'd have no time left to deploy the reserve.

He went for the three-ring release on his shoulder strap, the handle that would disconnect the main canopy from his harness, calculating that he would still have time to pull the reserve and make the landing comfortably.

He pulled the handle and waited for the sensation of total freefall to occur again as the canopy detached; but the feeling never came, and he realized that the release had failed too, that the lines and canopy were still attached, twisting worse than ever now, turning him with them, and his stomach lurched once more as he thought the rig might wrap itself around his body, which was plummeting ever faster to the forest below.

His hand, resisting the fierce wind, went to his leg and grabbed the hook knife attached to his leg strap, reaching upward and hooking it into the lines, cutting them one by one, the blade shearing through them cleanly, until the whole thing was finally released, sailing through the sky away from him.

He looked down, saw the rainforest canopy close now, so close, rushing up to meet him, to crush him, and he realized he would have no time to release the equipment he carried onto its wire; he was too low now, the pack might hit the trees before he'd even got the secondary chute open, and if it got caught in the canopy and then the canopy opened, his back might get broken by the snapping action, like a breadstick.

His pulled the release anyway, then cut through the wire as soon as it left his body, disconnecting it from himself entirely; and then, with the treetops almost within reach beneath him, he pulled the secondary chute, praying that it would work, and his body wouldn't be smashed to pieces by the rainforest.

But then the chute filled with air and arrested his

descent with the exact violence that had been missing from the first, and when he looked up and checked the canopy he saw it was intact; but he had no time to breathe a sigh of relief, as he saw he was about to hit the treetops.

Five seconds . . .

He scanned for a break in the trees, all too aware that the equipment was no longer there to break its way through first.

Four . . .

He saw nothing, just an expanse of wild *green*, coming up fast, too fast . . .

Three . . .

He saw something, instinctively steered the chute toward it.

Two . . .

He identified the small gap he'd seen and tensed his legs, pointed his toes, and hoped for the best.

One . . .

He hit the treetops hard, the impact tearing through his body, but he kept as tight as he could, like a diver entering the water and suddenly he was through the canopy, heading for the ground below.

And then his rate of descent slowed even more as the chute hit the canopy too, and started to get snarled and snagged on the branches above, until – finally – he came to a stop, dangling eighty feet above the rainforest floor.

Chapter Two

Lee felt his body swinging gently between the huge trees, and took a deep breath, calming himself after the highly adrenalized drop while he started to assess the situation.

He was alive, which was the first thing he had to recognize. Always the positives first. He checked himself over as he dangled in the air, glad to find that he had no significant injuries, in terms of broken bones, at least. But he had some open wounds, scrapes and gashes where the treetops had cut him on the way in, and he knew that such minor wounds could turn into life-threatening conditions in the rainforest if they weren't quickly treated and covered. Bacteria was rife here, in the hot, moist conditions; and so was every other form of life, Lee reminded himself as he started along the nearby branches for snakes or other animals which might be dangerous.

Jaguars were the apex predators of the Amazon, but he knew they wouldn't be found so high up in the trees. They could climb, but not like the leopard, and this was *because* it was forest's apex predator; whereas the leopard had to climb in order to hide its kills from larger predators such as the lion, the jaguar had no such competition. The shortness of its tail in comparison indicated that climbing wasn't as important. But there was always the exception that proved the rule, Lee reminded himself as he scanned the branches for the well-camouflages jungle cat; because if here was one up here, it would make his day go downhill real fast, even more than it already had done. With a bite strength more than twice that of a lion, the jaguar didn't have to latch on to the throat to suffocate an animal – it just bit straight through the skull.

Snakes were a lot more likely to be close by though. The real giants, like the Anaconda and Boa Constrictor, were found closer to the ground, and often near or in the water; but up here, the Emerald Tree Boa and the Amazon Tree Boa were both common, and highly dangerous. Many monkey species could be highly aggressive too, and meeting a group of them could well prove fatal. And then there were poisonous spiders, and a host of horror-inducing insects, as well as the highly-toxic tree frogs.

But after a long period of quiet observation, there was nothing he could see; and in fact, there was silence in the area directly around him, which was strange for an environment like this, which normally burst forth with sound. If it wasn't monkeys howling, or insects chirping, it was birds calling or predators growling.

Further out, Lee could hear the sounds, and realized that his crash landing must have scared away all of the animals close by.

He thought about the equipment he'd released, wondered if he'd find it; even with everything else that had been going on, he'd made a mental note of where it had fallen, so that he could retrieve it after landing. But that view had been from above, and he knew things would be much harder from the ground, where things looked very different. The major first aid kit was in the pack, but he had stashed a smaller one in the cargo pocket of his combat pants, and after getting out of the harness and getting to ground level, he would treat the cuts before they got infected, and then spend thirty minutes trying to find his equipment. After that, he would go it alone, with what he had with him. He knew how easy it was to fixate on something you thought you needed; he could start searching for the pack, lose track of time, and be caught out in the pitch darkness, with no idea where he was. And there was nothing in the pack – although the rest of his team would surely disagree – that he couldn't live without.

He didn't want to stay hanging in the trees forever, wanted to get moving, but he reached for the short-range radio he carried with him, knowing that getting through to Phoenix would be a lot more likely in the treetops than on the ground.

He noticed that it was turned off – maybe during the fall – and hit the switch, to immediately hear Phoenix's voice coming through.

"Echo-One," she said, "do you read me, over? Echo-One, do you –"

"Yeah," he said, "I read you."

"Oh, thank heavens you're okay, what are you doing?"

"Just hanging around," Lee responded, with half a smile.

Phoenix laughed nervously. "So, you're caught in the trees, right?"

Lee laughed too. "You got me."

"Anything broken?"

"No, but I lost the pack. I'll search for it when I get down, but I might not find it."

"You need to find it, you need –"

"I'll search for thirty minutes, and that's it. If it's not there, I'll just do this thing the old-school way, belt and braces. Did you see where I landed?"

"Yes," she said, giving him the estimated grid reference. He had a map and compass with him, and would check once he was down.

"We should come and get you," she said. "You can't possibly survive out there without that equipment, it's impossible for –"

"Phoenix," he said gently, "trust me. Like I told Silva, this is what I do."

"Okay, John. Be careful."

"You too," he said, before turning the radio off to conserve the battery.

He looked around him, from his vantage point suspended eighty feet above the forest floor.

Now all he had to do was find some damn way of getting down.

It was over twenty minutes before Lee was half way down the massive tree, secured to the trunk by the reserve parachute, which he'd adapted into a climbing rig.

He'd swung from the tangled lines of the reserve, back up in the tree canopy, getting enough momentum until he'd managed to reach the nearest branch that looked as if it could support him; and once he'd latched on, he'd cut himself free from the chute, then set about retrieving it from the treetops – which had taken a lot of time and energy, but could well prove life-saving. If he didn't find the pack, then the silk canopy and the lines would make a welcome substitute, as they were able to be used for a variety of purposes – climbing, protection, accommodation, the list was endless.

He'd made his way down through the branches and then – when the branches ran out, and it was just a long, straight trunk all the way to the ground – he'd used the parachute to get down the rest of the way, making a huge loop with the lines, which went around the trunk, and his back, the silk of the canopy adding some welcome padding. He'd leaned back into the rig, then walked down the tree, stopping every few steps to lower the loop. It had made the process of coming down much faster, and safer, than it would have been without, and he was happy that he would be safely down within the next few minutes.

But then he heard a noise, and stopped still. Voices, several of them, coming from below, further off into the rainforest.

Quickly, he shifted around the trunk, until his body was out of view from the direction he was hearing the voices come from. He knew that if anyone looked up, and was observant enough, they might see the white of the lines contrasted against the tree trunk; but they'd been darkened and dirtied after the climb, and were fairly thin, and he knew it would take a good eye to spot them.

He listened more closely as he sat there, leaning back into the rig, and thought he could pick up the sounds of Spanish.

Drugs gang, he thought immediately, presumably from the Peruvian side of the nearby border if they were speaking Spanish. Were they looking for him? He knew that such gangs operated a system of lookouts for planes and drones that might have been out searching for their labs, or drug smuggling routes, and had heard of more than one aircraft being brought down by rocket-propelled grenades or even surface-to-air missiles. They took their security seriously, that was for sure; and if they'd seen him parachuting into the forest, and happened to be close by, they would surely come looking for him.

He could hear their passage through the undergrowth now, and started to be able to make out some of the words. He wasn't fluent in Spanish, but knew enough to get by, and could certainly identify the gist of what the men were saying.

They *were* looking for him; and they were pissed off with being sent out to find him. The anger might work either way – on the one hand, it would take their mind off the job at hand, they were simply too busy complaining to one another to concentrate on actually finding him; but on the other, if they did find him, their anger would be instantly focused on him, and they were almost certainly armed with automatic weapons. And like anyone would tell you, anger and automatic weapons were *not* a good mix.

They became louder still, and Lee heard the foliage breaking on the ground beneath him, knew that they were coming into a position where they could see the lines, if they looked closely enough. From the voices and the sounds of their movement, Lee calculated that there might be five or six of them down there.

"This is a waste of time, man," one of them said, in Spanish.

"You're telling me," another said. "There must be a million trees in this freakin' area."

"Yeah," another said, so close to Lee's tree now, "but we found *this*, didn't we? If his pack's here, then *he's* here. Somewhere."

My pack, Lee thought. *They've got my pack.*

He wondered what they would make of it, what conclusions they would draw. There were no conventional weapons inside, but the sat-phone and mil-spec radio would – along with the parachute insertion – immediately make them think it was some sort of special ops insertion. It might seem strange that there was only one person, but they might assume they'd missed others, or there would be more to follow.

"Yeah, but where?" one of the men said.

"He could be watching *us* right now, man," said the first voice. "So get those rifles ready, okay?"

Lee breathed out, hoping they'd carry on past him; stuck thirty feet up a tree, he was a sitting duck.

"Hey!" one of the men said, and Lee was already reacting to the tone of his voice, hand going to his cargo pocket to pull out some of the cord he had cut away and not used for the climbing loop, his heart racing, "what is that?"

"What?"

"There, up there in the tree, around the trunk!"

Lee's hands were working furiously, tying the spare line off onto the loop, where it lay tight against the trunk. He was still thirty feet up, and there was only about twenty feet of line, but it would have to be enough; before the men had a chance to get around the tree, Lee had slipped free of the climbing loop and – holding the line near the end – he jumped straight down.

"Let's go!" he heard the shouts beneath him, along with the sounds of feet running, and guns cocking.

He was ten feet down when the first man raced around the corner, an old M16 in his hands. Lee let go of the line with one hand, withdrew his radio and hurled it down at the man, hitting him in his upturned face; and then the line pulled taut at the end of its length, the strain sending a sudden, shocking pain through Lee's shoulder, but he ignored it as he dropped the last few feet to the forest. Even though the line was ten feet short, because he'd held it at the end, the additional length of his body and outstretched arm meant that the unsecured drop wasn't too bad, and he landed lightly, grabbing the man's M16 and twisting it out of his hands, before smashing it into the guy's head just as two of his friends raced around the tree.

Lee jabbed the barrel of the gun into the throat of the first man, who dropped to his knees, clutching at his neck, struggling to breathe; and then Lee jumped up, standing on the fallen man's shoulder and planting a solid knee into the chin of the man who had been following close behind, sending him flying backward into the foliage.

The others couldn't be seen, and Lee realized they must have circled around the other side, to attack him from the rear; and without waiting for proof, he leaped to the side, just moments before the air came alive with the violent sounds of automatic weapons fire, Lee's back sprayed with chips of flying bark.

The tree was between them now, and it occurred to Lee that this was the old children's game, where one kid chased the other around a tree, feinting one way and then the other; only this time, there were at least two people to play against, and they had assault rifles, which made it a hell of a lot less fun.

Lee turned left, and withdrew as he spotted a man with a rifle, who fired after him; and like a kid, he feinted running back the other way, before going left again. The guy wasn't expecting him to be back this way, and ran straight into a high front kick, the heavy rubber sole of Lee's boot slamming him in the face and rocking his head back, knocking him out cleanly.

And now it was even more like the kids' game, one-on-one. Which way to go?

He waited and listened; and soon he could hear the sounds of ragged, scared breathing – definitely from just one person – along with the crack of twigs, around to his right.

Silently, his own breathing to a minimum, he followed the tree back around to the left, circling the trunk quickly but quietly, stepping over the bodies of the first two men he'd encountered and throwing a small rock back behind him to the right, to give the impression he was still there, or was moving in the other direction, *toward* the fifth man.

A few seconds later and he'd completed his circle around the trunk, could now see the back of the last man. "Estevez!" he shouted nervously. "You there, man?"

Three feet to go, and the man's head turned, eyes going wide as he saw Lee coming up behind him, moving the assault rifle around with him moments later.

Lee raced forward and kicked the barrel up, bullets bursting upward into the canopy above, the sound of gunfire followed by the loud squeal of monkeys and birds.

Lee reversed the direction of his leg and sent his

boot crashing down onto the top of the man's foot, cracking the bones as he fired an elbow into the guy's stunned face; and with the foot pinned, he fell straight back, pole-axed.

Lee wasted no time, but quickly gathered up the weapons and checked the immediate area, verifying that there had just been five of them. He went to the spot where they'd emerged, checking the tracks through the undergrowth made by their boots, and was satisfied, for now at least. But he knew there could be other teams in the area, who would have heard the gunshots and would even now be on their way here. The density of the rainforest might have blocked the sound, but he had to assume the worst, and work fast.

He took some of the vines that covered the area and tied the unconscious men up, so they couldn't pursue him; and then he went back to the assault rifles and removed their firing pins, rendering them inert.

He searched the men, but found nothing except for some cash and cigarettes; but then he discovered a radio on one of them, turned on. It gave him hope that perhaps other teams weren't in the area – for if they were, they would almost certainly have radioed through to check what was going on. He pocketed the radio, picked up his own backpack, and retreated to cover – further back into the rainforest, within a large clump of undergrowth that he first checked for snakes – in order to verify that everything was still in one piece.

It soon became clear that the drop had caused a lot of damage. The pack itself was torn in several places, but it was only when he checked the equipment inside that he realized how hard the impact must have been. The electronic equipment – the sat-phone, the radio, even the hardened laptop and GPS unit – were out of action, some of their inner parts spilling out. He tried them all, but not a spark of life remained. The first aid kit wasn't too bad, and he quickly dressed his wounds, cleaning and covering them as fast as he could.

The NVGs were gone too, and the water had leaked everywhere, but the rations and water purification tablets were okay, as were some of his more old-school weapons, which he pulled out and started to distribute about his person. It was, after all, looking more and more likely that he would need them.

It would have been good to get the parachute down, but going back up the tree to retrieve it was going to be more trouble than it was worth, and he decided to leave it.

He then took the broken equipment, dug out a hole in the moist earth within the undergrowth he hid in, buried it, and covered it. The he swung the pack – much lighter now – onto his back, and headed back toward the tracks the men had made through the forest.

He knew he was going to have to follow those tracks, back wherever the men had come from.

It was a no-brainer, really; Lee had parachuted into roughly the same area in which the university team had last been seen, and there was obvious drug activity in that very area. It didn't take a genius to put two and two together; if the team from Chicago had been here, they would definitely have been picked up by these guys. If Lee could find where they operated from, then he might even find the team – or at least, someone who might know where they were, or what had happened to them.

He used his own radio to try and get in touch with Phoenix and Marcus, but they were too far away now, and he couldn't get anything. He used his cellphone too, but – unsurprisingly – there was no reception here in the rainforest.

He put the radio and phone away, moved to the point where they had entered this particular area, breathed deeply of the warm, fetid air, and started to follow the tracks, wondering what he would find at the end of it.

Chapter Three

Tracking was a laborious process, and required almost supernatural levels of patience and observation. It might be a broken twig here, a small patch of flattened grass there; sometimes the only clue would be a smell that shouldn't have been there.

It was, he knew, why the most successful special ops guys in Vietnam had started to eat the same foods as the Vietnamese; before that, the enemy could literally *smell* the US troops coming.

It also reminded him of a rumor that jaguars had a particular liking for Calvin Klein's Obsession for Men, due to its use of civetone, a chemical extract that came from the scent glands of the civet, which was an animal the jaguar liked to hunt and eat.

In this case, however, the drugs boys had made things a little easier for him – they'd hacked their way through the undergrowth with machetes, and trampled the rainforest underfoot. The place was so alive that it was already starting to heal, to close down the passage left by the men, but compared to other trails he'd followed, this one was easy. After all, the men weren't trained professionals, or local tribesmen, and had made no effort to hide their route; and even if they'd wanted to, they'd probably lacked the ability, for moving through such terrain was a task as arduous and difficult as tracking, requiring the same qualities of patience and observation.

It still took considerable time to track the route to its source though, as he still had to move cautiously in case there were other teams about; and it always paid to look out for the natural threats of the rainforest, which were many and varied. During the time he followed the trail, he saw three different kinds of snake – thankfully from a safe distance – and had a much closer encounter with a six-inch long wandering spider, which held the distinction of being the world's most venomous. It was about to walk over Lee's boot when he spotted it, and he'd moved swiftly out of the way and let the little guy carry on. But in a place like the Amazon, you had to be constantly aware of everything around you, and it was a heavy strain on the system.

He had also had to respond to two calls on the radio he'd taken from the men, asking for updates on their progress. They had clearly not heard the gunfire, and also seemed to buy Lee's Spanish replies – although he helped himself by fiddling with the transmit button, causing the line to appear worse than it was.

The last call had been to advise the party to return to base, because night was drawing in, and Lee could see this was true; and in fact, by the time he had reached the place they'd set off from, night had fallen and it was completely dark.

This provided Lee with opportunities, but also presented problems. It meant he coud break into the compound – which on first appearance seemed to be a cocaine laboratory – and search for the university team; but it also meant that he'd lost his window of opportunity to set up his own camp for the night. It would be difficult to do it now, in the dark, especially as he knew he would be safer off the ground, up in the trees.

But, he supposed, he would have to just worry about that later; now it was time to see what he'd stumbled across.

An hour later, and he'd got a good impression of what he'd found. The compound covered an area of about twenty yards by twenty, and Lee noticed that they'd not cut down any trees to make space, obviously needing the canopy cover to protect them from aerial surveillance. They'd built around the tree trunks, although they'd cut down all of the low-lying vegetation. There was a bunk house, a kitchen and open-air dining area, and the lab itself. It was quite a big operation for such a location, and Lee was impressed that they'd managed to build anything at all. He supposed they would have had to drop supplies by helicopter, so remote was it from civilization.

There were twelve men in the camp that he'd

identified, four on sentry duty with M16s, the others sleeping in the bunkhouse smoking, drinking and listening to music in a central rec area. They kept the light levels low, and Lee knew that it was because they were worried that it would penetrate through the canopy above, and make them visible at nighttime, and he was impressed with their discipline. With no light from the stars or moon to guide him, it was a struggle to see the detail of the camp, and he actually found himself wishing that the NVGs hadn't been broken in the drop.

Such light levels meant that he could move around the camp unobserved however, and he made the most of the opportunity, checking it over inch by inch.

Search as he might, however, he could see that there was nobody in the bunkhouse, and no sign of the team from Chicago anywhere.

He retreated back outside the camp and wondered what he should do. Earlier on, when he'd first seen the place, he'd backtracked into the forest to radio the base, to say that his team wouldn't be back for another couple of hours, as they were finding it difficult to follow the track in the dark. The man he'd spoken to was concerned, asked if they had torches, and told them to be careful, and Lee didn't blame him; if the forest was dangerous during the day, then it was deadly at night. They certainly weren't going to send any men out to find them until morning. It gave him some leeway, but he wondered if the boys here would get suspicious if the recon team didn't come back. Would they eventually figure out what had happened, and break out all the weapons, for fear of a major attack on their camp?

He would rather wait until most of the men were asleep, but if he waited too long, they might get spooked and not go to sleep anyway; and then he would have twelve armed men to deal with, instead of just four. As it was, there were just the sentries with guns, and eight men relaxed and chilled out, in one area.

Yes, Lee decided, he would act now.

The team weren't there, and he could just move on, bypass the drugs lab and see if he could track the team some other way.

And yet someone there *might* know something, and Lee knew he had to question them if he could.

He also frowned strongly on the use of drugs, and – irrespective of his mission here in the Amazon – he wanted very badly to shut down the little operation they had going on here.

And – almost more importantly – it was nighttime, he had no camp of his own, and the beds in the bunkhouse looked *very* comfortable.

Chapter Four

Lee took the sentries out with the same blowpipe he'd used back in Utah. After all, he figured, if it ain't broke, why fix it? It was a motto he believed in, sticking with the tried and tested methods, and he'd been pleased when the pipe and darts had survived the crash landing.

It had seemed the perfect weapon to use in the rainforest at any rate, stalking up to targets through the undergrowth, like so many hundreds – perhaps even thousands – of generations of hunters before him, using the forest as cover before taking out the target with a single shot from the pipe. It connected Lee to his spiritual ancestors, humanity's near-lost hunter-gatherer past, and he felt as one with his surroundings as he moved around the camp, picking off the sentries, one by one.

But the sentries were the easy part, Lee knew, although he'd received a gift when one of the eight remaining men had wandered just outside the camp to urinate. Lee had pounced on the opportunity, dropping him with another poisoned dart, leaving seven in the central courtyard of the small compound to deal with.

He'd planned on creeping up on the men, keeping low as he stalked through the camp, but the gift of this guy leaving the compound was too good to pass up, and he quickly put on the man's shirt and cap, and picked up the rifle he'd carried out there with him – obviously SOP when leaving the camp.

Leaving his backpack next to the unconscious body, Lee stood and walked back into the compound as if he belonged there, mimicking the guy's half-drunk stumble, the cap pulled low over his face as he approached the others.

They sat under a tarpaulin, drinking what smelled like moonshine whisky from plastic bottles. A couple sat on upturned ammo crates, four more reclined in sun loungers, while the remaining guy was stood up, fiddling with the stereo, cursing the music that was playing.

They all had weapons nearby, Lee could see in the dim light of the single, low-wattage bulb that hung from a post that supported the canvas roof, but they weren't paying any attention to them. It looked like some of them had knives in sheaths on their belts, and the one standing up seemed to have a revolver stuck in the back of his pants, which meant that Lee had to assume everyone else had one too.

He wanted to get as close as he could to the group before it all kicked off, as he knew that the closer he was, the better chance he would have; if they spotted him from too far away, then they might have a chance to grab a gun and fire at him, which might make the day end even worse than it had begun.

But his confidence grew with each and every step he took, as he passed the lab, and came within a few feet of the small group of drug-runners.

One of the guys on the loungers, his eyes bleary, looked up at him. "Hey Rafi," he slurred, "what took you so long, eh? You know not to have a dump after dark, right? You don' want a jaguar biting you in the ass, man."

Everyone laughed, and turned toward him, and Lee knew the moment was upon him, that they would soon realize he wasn't Rafi at all; and so he moved, before they could.

He burst forward, swinging the butt of the M16 into the head of the man stood by the stereo set, dropping him to the ground as he spun the rifle around and brought it down like a sledgehammer onto the skull of the next man, one of the two sitting on the ammo crates.

The others were reacting now, and Lee snapped the barrel into the face of the man on the second crate, the hard metal breaking the nose, blood flying, black, through the dim light of the tent.

Lee spotted two of the men on loungers reaching for their rifles and jumped over to them, once more using the M16 as a club, cracking it across the first man's head while simultaneously burying his boot in the second man's face with a hard side-kick.

He saw another man pulling a pistol, and swiped

the M16 across, smacking the hard barrel across the guy's wrist before jamming the butt into his face; at the same time, he sensed movement behind him, saw the shadow of someone moving, and turned slightly, opening his hip fast and wide and sending a high hook kick whipping out toward the unseen target.

The impact wasn't perfect, Lee's calf connecting with the side of the man's neck, but it was enough to stun him, and Lee was pleased that it was, as the man was holding a knife with an eight-inch serrated blade, which he'd no doubt been about to plunge into Lee's back.

The scene was a confused mêlée, everything chaotic and brutal in the half-light of the solitary bulb; Lee was about to club another man who appeared in front of him, when he was tackled from the side by someone else, the impact knocking the gun from his hands. It would have taken him down to the floor, but Lee reacted to the movement instantly, secured a grip on the man with his now-free hands, and turned the guy over his leg and hip in a classic judo *harai goshi* throw.

With that man down, Lee saw the guy he'd been *about* to hit with the M16 now had his own rifle up, aimed in his direction; but instead of diving to the left or right, Lee jumped into a forward roll, the 5.56mm rounds ripping the night apart just above him, and as he came down from the roll, he let one of his legs straighten, smashing the heel of his boot down into the guy's groin in a rolling axe kick. He immediately switched onto his hip and lashed out with a round kick that sent the rifle spiraling out of the gunman's hands, came back with the same foot and smashed him in the knee with a side kick that dropped him low, and then quickly rolled onto his other hip and whipped out another round kick, this time connecting with the side of the man's head, knocking him unconscious.

Lee sensed movement next to him from the guy he'd thrown, and turned just as the man jumped on top of him, a knife now in his hands, forcing it down toward Lee's face.

Lee's hands went up to stop him, one on the man's wrist, holding the knife at bay, the other going to the guy's throat, gripping tight on the larynx. The eyes bulged above him, but the man was strong and held on, forcing the knife further down even as his other hand went to *Lee's* throat, going for the same move.

Instantly aware of the danger he was in, Lee lifted a knee sharply into the man's balls; it didn't stop him, but it was a distraction, and Lee felt the bodyweight shift above him. As it did, Lee's foot shot up into the space that had appeared between them, hooking into the inside of the man's leg; at the same time, he pulled and rolled backward over his shoulder, dragging the man with him in a circle until Lee lay on top, the attacker underneath him.

Lee dropped his head onto the guy's upturned face as soon as the roll finished, breaking the nose and making the man gag on his own blood; and while still distracted, Lee let go with one hand and slapped at the flat of the blade with his open palm, knocking the knife out of the guy's hand. In the next moment, Lee dropped an elbow into his startled face, but still the man was still conscious, using brute strength to turn away from Lee. Lee let him roll, releasing him just enough so that guy got onto all fours, escape the only thing on his mind, but then Lee pulled him back down, collapsing him to the floor, bodyweight crushing the drug-runner as Lee worked hardened, stiffened fingers down the line of the man's neck, until he could slip one of his forearm across, the throat placed in the crook of Lee's elbow, sides of the neck caught between forearm and biceps like a pair of pliers. His other hand went to the back of the guy's head then, first hand securing itself to the second arm's biceps, finishing the strangulation hold.

The man began to struggle, but it was too little, too late; the powerful hold cut off the blood supply to his head almost immediately, and Lee knew the guy was unconscious within the first few seconds. He left it on a couple of seconds longer, the body slack now, and then released him, standing slowly back up to survey the carnage.

Seven bodies littered the rec area, weapons, loungers and crates scattered across the little tented courtyard.

He breathed out slowly. Seven here, one outside, plus the four sentries made twelve total, seventeen if you included the guys he'd taken out earlier.

Even Lee had to admit, it wasn't bad for an evening's work.

***

Twenty minutes later, the men were all trussed up, secured and bound in a tight circle of bodies, sat straight-legged in the middle of the courtyard.

Earlier, he'd checked the men one by one, all too aware that one or more might still be conscious, might still go for a weapon; but they had all been out of it, and Lee had pulled their arms behind their backs as he went, pulling the shirts, vests or jackets down around their arms as makeshift handcuffs until he'd found something more substantial. A quick search of the camp had produced a roll of duct tape, and he'd gone back and done a better job of it.

By the time he'd finished, some of them were conscious, but they weren't going anywhere, not the way they were secured now. They were a captive audience, and Lee had some questions for them.

Once upon a time, he'd have taken them one by one into the bunk room for "enhanced interrogation", that painfully optimistic euphemism that the CIA had developed to cover up what amounted to torture. He had been part of that cycle at one stage, during his time with the agency's Special Activities Division, and the experience had changed him beyond all measure. What he had done, what he had been forced to do, had ultimately led to the destruction of his family, and a near-complete mental breakdown that had only been salvaged by his escape from the military, and his retreat to the monasteries of Thailand and China. He was getting better day by day, but it was still a work in progress, and he had no wish to be reminded of his time with the SAD by dragging these guys in for hardcore interrogation, drug-runners or not.

He would just ask them nicely, and hope for the best.

He walked around the group, the eight-inch serrated knife he'd picked up off the floor hanging loosely by his side. A picture, after all, was worth more than a thousand words, and just because he wasn't actually going to do anything to them didn't mean he wanted them to *know* that. The art of psychological warfare was pretty basic, at its heart. And wasn't it Roosevelt who'd advised to "talk softly, but carry a big stick"?

He'd already identified that four of the twelve were probably chemists, or what passed for chemists around here. They might not have had a technical job, might have been responsible for no more than crushing coca leaves with their feet, or mixing gasoline into the resulting paste; but the main thing was that they weren't cartel soldiers, were as close to ordinary working people as you could expect in this industry, and so might be more open to persuasion than the others, whom might have been inured to such things by a lifetime of death and violence.

He could see it in their eyes now – eight pairs were filled with anger and hate, and four pairs with fear and desperation. If he'd ripped the duct tapes from their mouths, eight men would have hurled every insult they could think of at him, would have threatened him with the vengeance of the cartels, while the other four might well have begged for mercy.

"Ladies," he said in Spanish, "I'm about to ask you some questions, and I would like some serious answers." He looked down at the knife in his hands, then back at the men as he continued to stroll around the circle. "If I don't like what I hear, I'm *not* going to hurt you," he said, and he could see the disbelief if their eyes. "But I *will* separate you from the group, and leave you outside the camp, tied up. A long way away, where no one can hear you scream." He smiled as he looked at them. "And you can't reason with animals, you know. Maybe you could make a game out of it? Guess what's gonna kill you first? Maybe it'll be a goliath tarantula, maybe a boa constrictor – you know, the ones that crush your bones, then swallow you whole? Or maybe a jaguar will give you a little kiss, plunge its teeth straight through your skull?" He shrugged. "Whatever it is, it won't be pretty. But as I said, *I'm* not going to hurt you.

"Now for my first question – the American research team that moved through this forest recently, where are they?"

He could tell there was something wrong as soon as he asked the question, as there was confusion on every face he could see – the genuine kind, when the person being questioned is actually caught out, and has no idea what they're being asked. Perhaps one person could have faked it, but not all of them, not all at the same time.

He approached one of the chemists, and pulled the duct tape from his mouth. "Talk," he said, although he already suspected what the man's answer would be. "Where are they?"

"I do not know what you are talking about," the man said, to Lee's dismay.

He believed the guy, but how was it possible? A group as large as the Chicago team moving through the forest wouldn't go unnoticed by such a group, as paranoid about security as they were. Hell, they'd been on him immediately, and there was only one of him. How had an entire team passed through without notice?

Unless this location was wrong, and they'd never been here at all.

"Two weeks ago," Lee persisted, "a team of eleven people – six Americans, five locals, they passed through this way. What happened to them?"

The man looked at Lee with fear in his eyes as he replied, scared that his unsatisfactory answers would result in being thrown to the jaguars. "Please," he said, "please. We were not even here two weeks ago, we are a mobile laboratory, we move location every month or so, you know, to avoid being found."

"When did you get here?" Lee asked, his heart sinking as he realized his hopes for an easy solution were quickly vanishing.

"Ten days ago," the man said. "Just ten days ago. Please. *Please.*"

Lee turned away, deep in thought.

Damn it.

Why couldn't they have just been in the bunk house, safe and sound? It would have made life *so* much easier.

"So you don't have any leads at all?" Lee heard Phoenix ask through the camp's powerful radio.

"Well," Lee said, "it's maybe not as bad as that. One of the guys *did* admit that they'd found a hat about six or seven klicks from here, when they'd been on their way in. American-made, which might not mean much, but it's something at least."

"You don't like coincidences," she said, reminding him of one of his mantras.

"Well, in this case I like 'em just fine," he said with a smile. "It's not much, but it gives me somewhere to start searching at least."

"You're sure they're not just blowing smoke up your ass?"

Lee laughed, having had exactly the same thought. "Maybe," he admitted, "but three different people pointed at the same location on my map, independently, so I'm gonna go with it."

"Unless it's a trap," Phoenix said. "Maybe another lab?"

Wow, Lee thought, *she's even more paranoid than I am*. "It's possible, but I don't think there'll be another facility so close. Nobody came running when the guns started going off, and they didn't speak to anyone else on the radio, as far as I can tell."

"Okay," Phoenix said, "then it definitely looks like a good place to start. What are the coordinates?"

Lee read them off to her, giving her a kilometer

grid square; between them, that was as accurate as three separate reports could be.

"A square kilometer?" Phoenix asked. "You're going to have fun tomorrow."

"Don't I know it," Lee said. "The hat isn't even there anymore, they picked it up."

Phoenix laughed. "No such thing as good luck, eh?"

"No," Lee admitted. "Not on this job, anyway. But I'll take a single square kilometer over a few thousand of them, any day of the week."

"Yeah," Phoenix agreed, "I guess so."

"Anyway, I'll go there in the morning, try and find some sign of them, and then follow the tracks, if I can find any." He paused, stretching his aching body. "And how about you guys? You settle in okay?"

"No problems," Phoenix said. "Got ourselves set up with a nice place. Not a hotel, a friend of Silva's; he's staying here too, keeping a low profile. Doesn't want to go back to Feijó yet, maybe not ever after escaping like we did."

"Understandable."

"He's on standby to help if he needs to," Phoenix continued. "Might be useful."

"Yeah. Any follow-up from the cops?"

"Not much," Phoenix said, "which might mean Rodrigues was in this alone, he doesn't want to tell other stations about the situation, because he doesn't want them asking questions. Still has his own men looking though, but nothing too heavy."

"Good," Lee said, happy that at least there was some good news today. "Any idea who killed Guzman?"

"Ah . . . yeah," Phoenix said, and Lee understood that all the good news had been used up. "There's something I need to tell you."

"Go on," Lee said cagily.

"It looks like there's a team from Apex in the area."

Lee's blood ran cold at the name. Apex Security Inc. was a private security force which took on contract work across the world, for the US government, foreign regimes, and any company who had enough money to hire them. Management didn't care who signed the checks, as long as someone did. They were a mercenary army in the worst way, like the Blackwater boys he'd come across during the wars in Afghanistan and Iraq, but with less scruples in how they operated.

They drew a lot of their active personnel from special ops guys, sometimes enticing them into discharging early with the promise of golden handshakes and huge bonuses. And they also targeted troops with questionable records, even those who'd been dishonorably discharged for misconduct; the way the management say it, they wanted dogs of war, and sometimes dogs didn't behave themselves.

"Do we know who hired them?" Lee asked.

"Not yet," Phoenix said, "but I'm working on it, okay?"

"Thanks," Lee said. "Now, I'll check in with you tomorrow morning before I leave, but I don't know when I'll be able to get in touch with you again. This radio's good, but it's too damn big and heavy to carry through the forest."

"You're sure?" came Phoenix's strained reply.

Lee looked at the radio, which resembled was roughly the size his entire backpack, and weighed in at around a hundred pounds. He *could* carry it – and maybe should, he knew – but moving through the rainforest was debilitating enough, without making it harder. If he was following tracks, he'd have to be mobile, and he'd be up and down constantly, checking for signs on the ground.

"I'm sure," he said. "But listen. You get Silva to fly over this area, over toward the Peruvian border, just after dawn and just before dusk, okay? If I need to communicate, I'll signal."

"Signal how?"

"The old-fashioned way, I guess. Smoke."

"The old-fashioned way, huh? That seems to be the way you like it."

Lee grunted, not sure if she was talking about mission tactics, or relationships, although she might have been right on both counts.

"He can drop a radio or sat-phone for us," Lee said, "if you can rustle one up."

"Yeah," Phoenix said.

"You might need to try rustling up a helicopter or two, as well," he added, "like we talked about."

"You don't ask for much, do you?"

"For the extraction," Lee said. "The forest's so

damn thick, there's no chance of using a plane to get those guys out, if I find them."

"I know, I know, we talked about it before. And don't worry, I'm already on it, I might have a couple of options."

"That's great. Now, I'm gonna get some sleep. You look after yourself, you hear?"

Phoenix laughed. "I will do. You too."

With that, Lee signed off and – giving his prisoners one last little check – he retired to the bunk house, to get some well-earned rest.

Tomorrow, he knew, was going to be a long day.

Chapter Five

Lee was up with the sun, and made himself a large breakfast from the food stocks in the small kitchen, before checking in with Phoenix again.

She hadn't learned any more about who'd hired Apex, but thought there might be as many as sixteen operatives in Brazil, still stationed in Feijó.

"What are you going to do with the people there?" she asked.

"I'm gonna let them go," he replied. After all, he wasn't a murderer. He'd even tell them where they could find their friends.

"And the lab?" she asked.

"Well," he replied with a grin, "we can't have this sort of place cluttering up the rainforest, can we?"

Daniel Forster drank a cup of strong black coffee and watched the sun as it rose slowly over the horizon, mesmerized by its beauty. It was going to be another beautiful day, he knew; and he could only hope that this time, it would have a satisfactory conclusion.

He'd been unable to control his laughter when Rodrigues had called him the day before, with news of what had happened in Feijó. An entire police department, undone by one man. But this wasn't, Forster had to admit, just any man. This was John Lee, the "Extractor" himself. The Feijó cops hadn't stood a chance.

It was a good pick the university had made, Forster had to admit. An ex-Delta Force man himself, he had great admiration for the work the PJs did, and he was impressed that Lee was transferring those life-saving skills to the civilian world. In a way, Forster was doing the same thing; only in his work for Apex Security, it was killing rather than rescuing that was required. Not as noble perhaps, but just as necessary.

"You found out where Silva and those others ran to?" he asked Ryan Millhouse, his intel specialist.

"Not yet," Millhouse answered. "But I'm sure we'll pick 'em up soon."

"Good," he said. He'd been tempted to kill Silva when he'd taken out Guzman; but his orders were clear, and whereas Guzman was a liability – he knew too much, and might well have informed other interested parties, intentionally or otherwise – Silva's piloting skills were actually needed. He was the obvious person for Lee to approach, and Forster had been pleased that things had gone as expected. Except for that business with Rodrigues; but the deputy commander had explained that Lee had accidentally seen the picture of

Guzman, and he'd been forced to do something.

That was fair enough, Forster could allow, but he'd had to stamp down on the man's desire to pursue things further. That wasn't part of the plans of Apex's employer, as Forster was quick to relay to Rodrigues. The man was stood down, for the sake of higher plans.

"Is the chopper prepped and ready to go?"

"Yes, sir," replied Jack Lightfoot, who'd once used to fly special ops missions with the famed Night Stalkers, the chopper pilots of the 160th Special Operations Aviation Regiment.

Forster nodded. "Good. Make sure you're good to go whenever we get the word."

Lightfoot confirmed the order, and Forster went back to drinking his coffee and watching the sunrise, foot tapping on the floor to a fast, incessant beat.

He'd been waiting too long and was itching for action, and he could only hope that the word would come soon.

An hour later, Lee was trekking through the rainforest, convinced he could still feel the heat of the explosion on his back.

The cocaine lab had lit up like a gigantic firecracker, the gallons of gasoline used to make the final product igniting fiercely. Lee wasn't worried that the fire would spread – the forest was simply too damp and moist for that – but the compound itself was incinerated.

Lee had been true to his word, and had let the

drug-runners go; only he'd also destroyed their radio, and had kept them bound in pairs, back to back. They *would* be able to escape, but it would take a considerable amount of time – time enough, hopefully, for Lee to make decent headway.

The most sensible thing, he knew, would have been to kill them all, to have incinerated them along with their laboratory. And in another time, another life, that was exactly what he would have done.

But he was a changed man, and he would never return to who he had been; that was the past, and had to remain buried. He knew the impulses still lay dormant somewhere within him, but he was winning the battle to keep them there, and had no intention of ever letting them out again.

The past slipped from his mind as he travelled through the vegetation of the rainforest, some lush and green, some rotting and near-black. He was assaulted on all sides by vivid sights and sounds – the brightly-colored birds in the trees, the insects crawling up the trunks toward them as colorful flowers competed with thick vines for space, monkeys calling and chattering from above, birds singing and screeching in the branches, insects chirping from everywhere. And then there was the moist, damp, oppressive heat, the sweat rolling down his skin, the mosquitoes that buzzed incessantly around him, the putrid smell of decay, and waste, and decomposition thick and heavy in the air.

The going wasn't too bad, as the lack of sunlight due to the canopy above meant that undergrowth at ground level was nowhere near as bad as that of secondary jungle, which could be almost impenetrable. But it definitely wasn't a running track, and progress was far from swift. On even ground, in good conditions, Lee could make a kilometer in under eight minutes without running, even with a heavy pack on his back; but here, he was looking at thirty minutes per kilometer, and – even though the drug-runners had made a passable trail on their way in – it was still exhausting work.

One of the biggest problems was the humidity, which was a real man-killer, even for someone who'd spent so many years in such conditions. It sapped the energy at an alarming rate, and Lee was glad that he'd managed to resupply his water from the compound. It weighed his pack down, but it was worth it; dehydration was one of the biggest dangers out here, and he knew he had to keep on top of it.

He also used water from the many vines he passed, careful to avoid those which exuded colored or foul-smelling sap but guzzling down the water contained in the good ones. It was sometimes sweet, sometimes bitter, depending on the vine, but it was enough to keep him going without the water he carried. Still, it was better to be safe than sorry, he knew.

Having said that, he was glad he wasn't carting that radio through the forest. If he was making one klick per half-hour with what he had with him, his pace would have slowed to a kilometer per hour or even worse, with the radio. He might not even have reached the target zone by nightfall.

As it was, it took him five solid hours of hard work to get to the rough location the men had indicated on the map.

The going was so slow not just because of the heat, but due to the necessity of keeping a constant watch of the surroundings for dangerous animals – including people – and terrain irregularities that could easily cause broken ankles or knees, something that would slow him *right* down. And then there was navigation, which was hard as hell in the rainforest, even with the semi-trail that he was following. He'd stolen a GPS unit from the compound, but never one to trust technology completely, he had been constantly cross-referencing it with his map and compass, to make sure he was definitely on the right track. The one thing he didn't want to do out here was to get lost.

Obstacles had made it harder too, making six klicks on the map into more than ten on the ground.

Five hours, he told himself as he pulled his pack off and sat down to eat some dried biscuits, was some achievement, however slow it had felt. It wouldn't be up there with the tribesmen who lived in the Amazon, but was probably twice as fast as most people would have managed over similar terrain, and had put him in his target location before midday, which left him several hours of daylight to locate some sign of the research team.

As he sat, he allowed himself to relax, ever so slightly; midday in the Amazon was probably the safest time of day. He was sheltered from the strong sun by the tree canopy, and many of the most dangerous animals hunted between dusk and dawn. But he knew he couldn't let his guard down entirely, because *anything* was possible.

He listened to the forest around him, taking it all in – the screech of the howler monkeys, the loud call of the macaws, the constant thrum of the cicadas and – somewhere far off – the grunt of a peccary.

After a few moments of straining to listen to the distant hog, anew sound came to him, one that had previously been drowned out by the rest. It was familiar, yet faint . . . so faint . . .

Listening to the world around him had been one of the skills he had learned in the Tibetan temple. The abbot of the monastery in Thailand had recommended the place to him, after Lee had been there for several months, because he thought the Tibetan temple might be the only place where Lee could find the answers he sought.

The abbot had been a monk of the famous Shaolin lineage, although he had spent almost his entire life at a subsidiary temple to the more famous one in Henan Province; as the abbot related it, the Henan monastery was for show, while the secondary temple, hidden in the mountains northwest of Chengdu, was where the real thing happened.

And so Lee had begun his pilgrimage to Tibet, a trek that had taken months; and when he had arrived at the temple, perched on the edge of a cliff in the frozen mountains, he was ready to learn.

THE EXTRACTOR

There had been a lot of physical training at the temple, as might have been expected in a place run by a master of Shaolin; but there had been even more time spent on meditation, both in movement, and stillness. Sometimes entire days devoted to listening to the world around him, attuning himself with nature, with the universe itself.

He tapped into that same feeling now, occupying that zone between consciousness and unconsciousness – or perhaps even super-consciousness – whereby he could *feel* the sounds around him, in his heart.

And, in a near-trance-like state, he rose, put the backpack on, and started to follow his heart, allowing it to take him where it willed, without question, without interference from his conscious mind.

He moved through the undergrowth quickly and confidently, guided by senses he didn't fully understand, until he came to a dense stand of trees he could barely get through. He kept trying, pushing harder and harder through the thick vines and cloying vegetation, until finally, mercifully, he burst through to the other side, the source of the sound now all too clear to him as he fell, exhausted, to the ground.

There was a waterway there, something between a large stream and a small river, the sound of running water almost all but block out due to the wall of trees that surrounded and sheltered it. It wound its way through the rainforest, its path completely covered from above due to its proximity to the trees, the canopy covering it completely. His consciousness returning, his mind coming back to reality, he recognized that it didn't appear on his map; and when he checked the GPS, he discovered that the battery had run out completely. Typical amateurs, he thought sadly as he tossed the unit aside, they hadn't even maintained their equipment properly. But anyway, Lee had to assume that this waterway was only known about locally, maybe only by the indigenous tribes, if there were any.

And yet he knew, instinctively, that it could be the route that the research team followed. It would make sense for a tribe to be located near a source of water, and it had confused him that the area being searched was so far from the obvious sources. A hidden river made perfect sense for a hidden tribe. The drug gang had passed within a few hundred yards of it, and probably never even realized it was there.

Lee wondered about his next course of action. He didn't have any evidence – yet – that the party had come this way, and the logical, trained part of him told him that he should go back to the grid square he was supposed to check, and look for definite sign of the research team. However, he also knew that he was now off the trail set by the drug-runners, and – without the GPS to tell him where he was – he might never make it back. His run for the river had been in a state of near-catatonia, and he had no memory of the route he had taken. If he managed to get back through the trees, he might be able to pick up his own trail, but he might not; and he could easily waste previous hours looking for something be might never find.

Navigation through a rainforest wasn't so hard if you knew where you were starting from; but with an inability to see more than a few yards in front of you at any given time – and sometimes much less – it was nearly impossible to use the traditional method of triangulation to establish location. If he found some high ground, he might be in with a chance, but even if he did, it would likely be covered by trees anyway.

On the other hand, if he followed the river, it gave him something concrete to do. He might still be wasting his time, but at least he had a chance. Logically, he knew that people stayed near water, and this was as good a chance as any; but more important than that, his *gut* told him it was the right thing to do.

His mind made up, he looked up and down the wide stream and thought about how he was going to do this.

He would follow the river west, toward the Peruvian border, knowing that this was the direction the team were headed in. But how would he follow it? He could try and trek along the bank, which is probably what he would have done under normal circumstances if he didn't have a boat; and yet the trees lined the river so closely, that there wasn't really any bank to speak of. Another option was to push back beyond the line of trees, and follow the trees from the other side, hoping that they continued to follow the path of the river. But he knew that they might not, and such a method might only end up getting him very lost, very quickly.

A third option, of course, was to get in and swim,

but there were all sorts of dangers associated with that. Anacondas, caimans, piranha, leeches, and – perhaps the most disturbing of all – the *candiru*, a parasitic catfish that was known to force its way up the urethra of unsuspecting swimmers. Give him an army of caimans any day of the week, Lee thought.

And yet, he also knew that swimming would be the fastest method by far, especially as the current was heading in the right direction. He would use the backpack as a flotation device, resting his arms and upper body on it as he kicked downstream with his legs. It was lined with a waterproof bag, so he knew that what remained of his equipment would survive.

He looked one last time at the tree line behind him, then back at the fast-flowing waters in front.

And then he slung the pack off his back, and jumped in.

Chapter Six

The current took him fast down the waterway, and – despite the dangers of hitting submerged rocks – it suited him just fine, as it meant he was much less of a target for predatory animals. Besides which, if he hit a rock, the backpack would take most of the impact.

He tried to observe the world around him as he was swept downstream, but it was harder than he imagined, as the warm water crashed and splashed over the pack in front of him, blinding him for half the time; while during the half he *could* see, he was too busy steering himself through the churning rapids or looking out for passing caimans.

But he got vague impressions of the passing rainforest, the main one being how strange it was to be in a river, completely shielded from the sun by the thick canopy overhead; for no matter how far he went, the waterway never widened enough to come out of the shade, and the trees continued to hug the river tightly, keeping it almost bankless all the way. It never seemed to narrow too much either, and kept a fairly uniform width throughout his journey, which in itself was strange. It was like a river from another world, and Lee wondered how many people had ever seen it.

He checked Darrow's watch – happy that, after everything he'd been through, it was still attached to his wrist – and was surprised to see that he'd been in the water for nearly two hours. How far might he have traveled in that time? He had no idea, no idea at all. Five klicks? Ten? Twenty? He might even have just been going around in circles, he had no idea of the route this river took; even now, he might only be a few hundred yards away from where he started. And yet he had the feeling that a lot of distance had been conquered, far more than he would have covered by marching through the forest itself.

And the further he traveled, the more he began to think this whole insane story about a lost tribe, immune to illness and disease, might actually be true.

If he ever got there in one piece to find out, however, was a different matter, he thought as he finally hit one of the submerged rocks with his backpack, an impact that sent him spinning out toward the trees that lined the river. A moment later and he bounced into the underwater bank, and span back toward the central channel, choking on the warm river water that crashed over him with escalating violence, and Lee realized he was being pulled toward a whirlpool, now just a few yards away.

He struggled against it, fought it, but it had already

caught his backpack in its outer spiral, and it was dragging him in, relentlessly, against his will, and he was powerless to stop it . . .

He let go of the pack, sacrificing it to the power of the vortex, and he immediately started to use his arms to swim too, pulling hard, driving ever forward, kicking free of the pull of the whirlpool until he was out of its deadly embrace at last, exhausted but alive, and he let the current just take him as he relaxed slightly, the tension in his muscles ebbing away slowly as he drifted peacefully for a few glorious moments, basking in his continued survival.

But then he felt the current's pull increase, and adrenaline spiked through him once more as he rounded a bend and realized he was being carried toward a vanishing edge, which could only mean . . .

Waterfall.

He reached out desperately for something to hold onto, a floating vine, or the roots of the nearby trees, but he couldn't reach them, couldn't make it that far, the edge was coming up too quickly, and all he could do was relax his body and allow the river to take him over, praying he would not be killed on the other side.

The breath was forced out of him as he dropped, the water crashing all around him, the tree canopy still covering the sky as he plummeted downward, ever downward; and in a moment of crystal clarity, he saw everything – the rainforest looming high around him, the boulders lining the waterfall, the passage of water twenty feet down to yet more boulders blow, the water crashing against them, the same way *he* would crash against them moments later. It looked to be that a messy death was all but inevitable, that his body would be dashed to bloody pieces on the rocks below; but in that same moment of clarity, of heightened awareness, he saw his way out.

He allowed his body to fold as he fell, angling slightly, sweeping toward the boulders at his side; and then he hit them with flexed ankles, bent knees, water rushing everywhere about him, using them as a platform to spring forward, to jump as far as he could, clear of the raging torrents below, and he prayed he had jumped far enough as his body plummeted through the air, until he made impact . . .

But it was with the water alone, the boulders and the crashing waterfall less than a yard distant, and he gathered his remaining energy and swam forward, pulling himself clear of the small but deadly cascade, into the calmer, more still waters of the lower river, where he allowed himself to float as he forced himself to breathe, to breathe, to . . .

And then he saw them, half-hidden in the foliage.

Men, by the side of the river, semi-naked, spears held high, eyes threatening as they observed him silently drifting down the waterway.

Out of the frying pan, he sighed to himself internally, *and into the fire* . . .

CHAPTER SEVEN

Lee walked down a narrow trail through the forest, clothes and shoes soaking wet, all of his weapons and equipment lost; ahead and behind him were three tribesmen, all armed with short, javelin-type spears. From their appearance – tall and lean, teeth gleaming in the weak forest light – Lee could only surmise that he had found the tribe he'd been looking for. Or, rather, they'd found him. The only question now – other than if they were marching him somewhere just to execute him in a more dramatic or ceremonial location – was whether the research group had also found them.

He hoped he would soon find out.

The tribesmen – who he'd at first expected to throw their spears at him, a sitting duck in the water – had thrown vines in for him, and helped to pull him out. They'd not spoken to him, perhaps realizing he wouldn't understand them, and they had merely encouraged Lee to fall into step with them through only the very feintest of gestures with their sharply-tipped spears.

Back in the water, Lee had considered swimming to the other bank, but he thought they would only follow him, and be angry when they caught him. He'd also thought about going on the attack when they pulled him out, but his hand was stayed for two reasons – one, that they'd just helped him; and two, that he needed them. If they were who he thought they were, then he wanted to go wherever they were taking him, as the people he was searching for might – just *might* – also be there, and he couldn't pass up the opportunity to find out.

Lee couldn't believe how densely packed the trees were in this particular area, and understood why these people had managed to remain hidden for so long. For oil prospectors and loggers, the area was – for the time being, at least – too remote to make profitable, too difficult to explore properly. And for the gangs looking for drug-running routes, or locations to set up hidden labs, there was a fine line between a location which was hidden, and one which was all-but-inaccessible.

Lee wondered where they were going, and how long it would take to get there; what light there was, was starting to fade, and he knew dusk would be upon them soon. Due to the canopy, days inside the rainforest could be surprisingly short, with darkness falling regularly by four o'clock.

They came to a stop only a few moments later, and for the first time, Lee could hear the familiar sound of voices – adults chatting, children crying and laughing, the noises distant and faint but definitely recognizable.

They were too distant to make out words, but there seemed to be a mix of dialects and speech patterns – one definitely indigenous, tribal and barely recognizable, the other much more familiar.

It was the strident, confident and entirely familiar tones of Americans.

Yes, he thought, listening harder, and with growing excitement, *it has to be!*

But where were they? He couldn't see anything through the tightly-packed trees, couldn't make out anywhere that might be a camp or village. And yet the sounds were growing louder, the voices clearer, and they seemed to be coming now from all around him.

Where *were* they?

And then Lee sensed sudden movement above him, and he pivoted clear as a vine dropped into the space next to him, others dropping nearby, in close proximity. The nearest tribesmen looked at Lee with what appeared to be a smile, as if to congratulate him for avoiding the vine, and then pointed upward.

Lee followed the finger, and traced the exceptionally long vines as they wound their way upward into the treetops, where he could also see . . .

Damn.

Huts. There were damned *huts* up there, in the trees, and Lee suddenly understood another reason why this tribe was all but unknown.

The sound of American voices filled him with hope, that the people he had traveled so far to rescue were still alive, against all the odds.

Subconsciously, he touched the watch that Darrow had given him, wondering if he was going to get a chance to give it to Lisa Garfield, as a symbol of love, of hope, of emotions and feelings that were so desperately needed in the world.

The three men in front of him tucked their spears away into the belt-type garments they wore from shoulder to hip, which strapped the weapons to their backs, leaving their hands free to climb, and Lee watched as they started to pull themselves up the surrounding trees, planting their feet against the trunks and walking as they went hand-over-hand on the vines.

The man who was still stood next to him gestured upward again, and Lee knew that was his instruction to follow the others. And so he took hold of the vine that had almost hit him – presumably thrown down by the villagers above – and started to climb.

Although he knew he should be nervous – he had no idea what was waiting for him up there – the fact was, he couldn't wait to find out.

When Lee got to the top, arms and shoulders aching from the climb, he took in the surroundings as quickly as he could, all too aware of the failing light. The area was a treetop village, huts linked by walkways suspended beneath the canopy, maybe seventy or eighty feet above the forest floor. It was an incredible sight, and even if he was killed now, he was glad to have seen it.

Not that he had any intention of letting them kill him, of course; if they tried, they'd soon regret it, even outnumbered as he was. But even though the men kept their spears on him, he didn't get the impression that they were desperate for a confrontation; rather, it was for self-defense, and they were taking precautions with him until they could establish who he was, and what his intentions were.

It was hard to make out who was who, people spread out throughout the treetops in individual huts, some large, some small, all obviously serving some sort of purpose for the community. Although he couldn't immediately see each structure, he imagined there must be residential huts, places for cooking, perhaps even some sort of areas that served ceremonial purposes.

The other men came up behind him then, and – the six-man escort once again complete – they gestured with their spears, and continued the march.

Lee walked across the platform they'd climbed onto – obviously the main way in and out of the camp – and across a narrow and precarious-looking bridge to the next tree along, which housed a hut that Lee soon realized was a security center, almost like a border post.

Two hard-eyed, angry-looking men regarded him coolly, looking him up and down, before speaking to the escorts. One of the men responded, and a brief, violent discussion ensued that Lee couldn't understand a word of. But eventually, one of the security men turned and left the hut out of the opposite side, venturing deeper into the elevated village.

Lee waited with the others in silence, wondering if the man had gone to get a more senior tribal member, maybe even the chief himself, if this group had one. Hell, they might have a working parliamentary democracy for all he knew.

Five minutes later, the man returned, and it wasn't with the chief; instead, the person he had with him was white, American, female, and well-known to Lee from the file Dunford had provided.

It was Gale Rhodes, team leader of the expedition, and Lee's heart soared when he saw her, final confirmation that he was in the right place, that the team – or part of it at least – was still alive.

PART THREE

Chapter One

"Gale," Lee said as he saw her approach, "thank heavens you're alive."

"American?" she asked, eyes opening wide.

Lee nodded, and she burst forward, hugging him tight, despite his bedraggled appearance. He hugged her back, or tried to, at least; but at a nod of the security guards, two of the spearman moved forward and separated them.

"I've been sent by the university," Lee said, before he could be silenced. "To get you."

Gale looked at him doubtfully, eyes roving up and down. "You?" she said, and Lee didn't take offence. He realized how it looked. "Just you?"

Lee shrugged. "University budgets are tight these days, I guess."

Gale laughed, and the sound was pleasant; but the guards started barking at her, and she soon stopped.

"They want to know why you're here," she said.

"You understand them?" Lee asked. He knew from

her file that – in addition to her medical qualifications – she was a formidable linguist who had already spent some time with the indigenous tribes of Brazil, one of the reasons that she had been selected as team leader.

"A little," she said. "What I've managed to pick up since we've been here, however many days that is. It has some similarities to a couple of other so-called 'uncontacted' tribes in the area, but it's fairly unique, actually."

"Ten days," Lee said.

"What's ten days?" Gale asked.

"Since your last contact. Ten days."

"Hm. Seems a lot longer, somehow. It –"

There were more barks from the guards, and Gale spoke back to them in the same fashion.

"Don't worry about them," she said. "Their bark is worse than their bite. Although . . ."

"What? Is everyone on the team still okay?"

"My team is," Gale said. "A couple of them are injured, another one ill with dysentery, but still alive."

"The guides?"

"They're gone," Gale said. "They left when we met the tribe, thought it was bad luck to stay. They're walking, they're probably not even home yet."

"They know where this place is?" Lee asked.

Gale shook her head. "They got us as far as the river, then left," she said. "That was enough for them."

"The hunters?" Lee asked next.

Gale shrugged. "Well, I know I said their bark is worse than their bite, but . . . well, they do have tempers. But then again, when they met us on the river, the hunters did what their instincts told the, I suppose."

"They went for their guns?"

Gale nodded. "And they both ended up with several spears sticking out of them. The rest of us were pretty compliant after that."

"I bet."

There were more questions from the guards, and Gale responded. The conversation – strained due to the lack of a common language – lasted quite some time, but eventually Gale turned back to him.

"I told him who you were, that you've been sent to take us back. But they're a suspicious lot, as you can tell, so a higher authority needs to get involved."

"I'm going to meet the chief?" Lee asked with a smile.

"Yes," Gale confirmed with a smile of her own, "you're going to meet the chief."

The chief's hut was indeed the nicest – and largest – that he'd seen, and the man even had a throne of sorts, a small hammock-seat made of interwoven vines.

The man was about forty, and in rude good health. He had no adornments that marked him out as chief, but everyone was clearly subservient to him, respecting whatever authority he wielded.

"He welcomes you to his village," Gale said, after a barked greeting from the chief.

"Please tell him that it's an honor to be here," Lee said, and listened as Gale translated for him.

The chief spoke again. "He asks, if you're here to rescue us, how do you intend to get us back home?" Her eyes twinkled. "And I must admit, I was kind of curious about that myself."

"Helicopter," Lee said, hoping that it was true.

"How will it find us?" Gale asked, once again translating for the chief.

"He knows what a helicopter is?" Lee asked.

"We've had some cultural exchanges," Gale answered. "He gets the basic idea, anyway."

"Well," Lee said, answering the chief's question, "we've got a plane sweeping the area twice a day. Now that I've lost my communications, I'm going to signal it with smoke, and then they'll drop us a radio or satphone to our location. We'll then make a call, and wait for extraction."

She translated for the chief, seeming to struggle with most of the words and having to resort to hand gestures for some of them. "Where will it land?" Gale asked next, a question of her own, the chief not having spoken.

"We might have to get winched up," Cole admitted. "Landing pads are in short supply around here, unfortunately."

"Tell me about it," Gale said with a smile.

The chief spoke again. "He says you are welcome to leave at any time, as are we. He only asks that we make the signal from outside the boundaries of the river, on the far side and well away from this location."

"Tell him that this will be no problem."

Gale translated, and the chief smiled, clapped his hands, and spoke again. "He also says that there is nothing more to be done tonight, as the sun will be down soon and we can't go anywhere, and so he asks you to stay as his guest, and eat with us."

"Please tell him that he is very kind, and it would be my honor to accept."

After a day like this, Lee told himself, some food and rest would be *very* welcome.

Chapter Two

"Where are the other two?" Lee asked as he sat cross-legged on a large platform that seemed to function as a communal dining facility. There was a fire in the middle, and Lee sat with Gale and another three members of the research team, with other members of the tribe stretched around the platform in a large circle, the chief sitting between them.

"Lisa has dysentery," Gale said, "and Jake's looking after her. He's one of the injured ones, he's got a broken ankle and he's finding it pretty hard to get around."

Lee nodded his head, hand going reflexively to the watch when he heard Lisa's name. He knew he would have to go and see her after dinner, tell her that Sylvia hadn't forgotten her.

"How's she doing?" Lee asked, concerned that she would struggle with the extraction, if it involved being winched up into a helicopter. It had already been decided with the chief that he would be taken at first light to a safe location where they would help him signal

Silva. Lee assumed that – if Phoenix and Marcus were on top of things – he'd already have the sat-phone or radio with him, and it would be dropped immediately. With the help of the locals, he would find the drop-site, radio or call through to Phoenix, and arrange the chopper extraction for that same day, if possible.

"Getting better," Gale said.

"Good. How about Jake? Do you think he's gonna be able to make it to the chopper?"

Gale shrugged. "He's going to need some help."

Lee nodded. "You said you had two injured. Who's the other one?"

"Eva," Gale said, motioning past the flames of the roaring fire at a woman sitting on the other side. "Ligaments in her knee. She's getting around on a makeshift crutch, but again, she's going to need help."

"Okay," Lee said, gesturing at the tribe members sat around the open dining area. "We might be able to get some of these guys to help us. If not, we'll have to do it ourselves."

Gale nodded. "We can do that," she confirmed.

Lee was presented with a plate made of thick leaves, a mixture of fruit and fresh fish on it, presumably caught from the nearby river by the guys with the spears. He smiled and gratefully accepted it, picking up the food with his fingers and tucking in, the villagers looking on in approval.

"It's good," Lee told Gale in between mouthfuls.

"We can't complain," Gale said. "They've been good hosts. Well, since they killed those two guys, anyway."

"So, what happened, anyway? Where's your equipment, your radios?"

Gale received her own leaf-plate and took a mouthful of fish before answering. "The tribespeople destroyed it," she said. "The fact was, they didn't trust it. They found us in a boat on the river – the guides had packed inflatable canoes, which we carried through the forest – and the two guys from Manaus went crazy, grabbed their guns and started shooting. The tribesmen scattered, then came back and counter-attacked with arrows and spears."

"Yeah," said another of the group, who Lee recognized as Stephen Roberts from the file photographs, "we thought we'd had it, man, we really did. We were terrified."

"Probably the worst few minutes of my life," Eva added. "In fact, not just 'probably'. *Definitely*."

"It's lucky they were such good shots," Gale said. "They killed the hunters, and then -maybe seeing we didn't have weapons – they left us alive."

"But that first hour, we were all convinced we were going to be killed," commented the last member of the research team by the fire, Greg Karlson, "just the same as the hunters, spears and arrows sticking out all over us like pincushions."

"There was a lot of shouting," Gale remembered, "and they broke and smashed everything we had with us – radios, phones, supplies, medical kits, research equipment, computers, GPS, *everything*."

"I remember thinking," Karlson said, "that they might as well have killed us. I mean, without comms back to the outside world, how they hell were we ever going to get back? How the hell was anyone ever going to find us?"

"How *did* you find us?" Eva asked.

"Luck," Lee had to admit. "A bit of planning, but a lot of luck."

"But there's just one of you," Roberts observed, "and you've got no equipment or supplies either. I mean, what's the plan?"

Lee outlined it for them, and they all sat in silence for a few moments as they considered it.

"Well, hell," said Karlson eventually. "It's better than nothing, right?"

Everyone laughed, nodding in agreement. "Yeah," Gale agreed, "it's definitely better than nothing. Although a part of me wishes we could stay longer."

"Oh?" Lee asked with raised eyebrows.

"I mean, we still haven't really fully understood what we're looking at here."

"In what way?"

"Well, you know the chief?" she asked, pointing through the flames.

Lee nodded. "Yeah."

"How old do you think he is?"

"Forty, maybe."

"Try nearer seventy," Gale answered.

"Seventy?" Lee sputtered, unable to believe it. "Damn, the old boy looks good for his age."

"Doesn't he, though? And it's the same story throughout the village. Everyone's in great shape, no matter their age. In fact, they don't even really think about age in the same way that we do, it simply doesn't affect them as much. Sure, they die eventually, but it's generally when they're *very* old, and almost never through disease or illness, which – the rumors are true – just don't seem to affect them. We've checked them out thoroughly – or as thoroughly as they'll allow us anyway, and without the equipment to do proper tests – and they just seem to be resilient, you know? To *everything*."

"Any idea why?" Lee asked. "Or how?"

"They claim – and it might well be true – that their health stems from ingestion of a certain type of flower, which they include as a major part of their diet."

"A flower?" Lee asked.

"Yes," Eva replied, pointing to the trees above them. "If you can believe it, it grows above the canopy, or at least in the upper reaches of the canopy, as part of these trees."

"The flowers grow *on* the trees?"

"They seem to," Eva replied, and he remembered that she was the plant specialist on the team. "We're not sure if it's actually a part of the tree, or if it's a separate thing, perhaps some sort of symbiotic relationship. But I've never seen anything quite like it. I've collected some samples, when we return to Chicago I'll start finding out more about them. It looks a little like a bromeliad, but I think it's closely related to the orchid family."

"And you think it has some sort of medicinal

properties?" Lee asked.

Eva shrugged. "I've got no equipment hear to establish that. But take a look around you, take a look at these people. There's something going on, and this flower is the only thing that is significantly different from the diet of other tribes. Now, it might be from ingesting it, or it might even be from breathing in the pollen, they're so close to the flowers up here, we just don't know. We're going to have to come back, though."

"Come back?" Lee asked in surprise.

Gale nodded her head. "Oh yeah. We need to scientifically evaluate this, we need our equipment, our instruments. Any samples we take back are going to be incredibly helpful, but we need to investigate on-site. In fact, I'm thinking of staying."

"You're *what?*"

"Look," Gale said. "We know where this place is now, right? We have links to these people. Now, why don't you take the injured and ill – that's half the team – back to the US, and leave us here. Eva can take the plants she's found to the lab and start work on the testing, and – if we can arrange to have our equipment dropped – then we can wait for it here, and do some serious work."

"Won't these guys just break it all again?" Lee asked.

Gale shrugged. "I know some of the language now," she said. "I think I can communicate our needs to the chief, explain why it's important. And if they break everything? Well, at least you know where we are now, you can just come and get us."

"Oh, I can?"

Gale shrugged again. "Well, someone can, anyway."

"I admire your dedication," Lee said. "But how do these guys feel about it? The more you keep pressing this thing, the more likely it is that the tribe will be discovered. And then what? Everyone will want a piece of them, won't they?" he shook his head. "Their way of life will be destroyed forever."

Gale sat in silence for a few moments, deep in thought. "Yes," she said. "You're right. It's selfish, it could cause this tribe to lose a way of life it's lived for . . . well, who knows how long? But think about it – can we pass up this opportunity? What if this flower – or something else here – does offer the prospect of complete immunity?" She waved her hand around the village. "How many people live here? Fifty, maybe? What we want to do is to take some samples, do some investigating, some research. It is a risk, maybe it will mean everyone here will have to change the way they live, to join the rest of us in the wider world. Yes, it's possible. But if what we have here can help millions – perhaps *billions* – of us to reap the same sort of rewards as this tribe, then how can we not do that? With a gift so magical, is it not more selfish to keep it here for just fifty people?"

Lee picked up some fruit and ate it as he thought about what Gale had just said. He knew that she was right, to a certain extent at least. It was true that a lot of people might benefit from whatever was found here. And yet, wasn't the justification of the "greater good" the excuse every tyrant in history had made? How many people had been killed over the years, how many civilizations and peoples had been lost for all time, in the pursuit of the "greater good"? It smacked of hubris, of arrogance; and yet Lee also knew that – as night followed day – such processes were inevitable. This tribe was inevitably going to be brought out into the open one day; once a single person knew about it, once the secret was out of the bag, then that was it. And that moment, he knew, had already passed.

"Well," Lee said noncommittally. "You're the scientists. I guess you guys know best, right?"

She gave him a sour smile in return, and went back to eating her fish.

"I'm going to go and see Lisa and Jake," Lee said, pushing himself up from the floor. "Tell them what's going on."

"Good idea," she said. "I'll come and see them too, when I've finished."

"I'll tell them."

Lee headed out from the dining platform, following directions he'd been given earlier. It was dark out here now, especially after being close to the fire, but there were occasional torches to light the way as he walked gently across the narrow bridges and walkways that connected this marvel of native architecture. He passed several other huts, all with families in them; some waved, others just stared, but nobody seemed aggressive or threatening, or displeased to see him in their village. There was some suspicion, perhaps, but nothing more.

Finally, he got to the hut where Lisa and Jake were staying, and poked his head around the corner. "Can I come in?"

Jake Harwood looked at him and nodded. "You're the guy come to get us out of here, right?"

"Right," Lee confirmed.

"Yeah, the others told me about you. Of course, you can come in. But be quiet." He pointed at a body on the floor, fast asleep on a bed of palm fronds. "She's out of it."

Lee looked down and saw Lisa Garfield, and he thought again of Sylvia Darrow, how heartbroken she had seemed when she even considered the thought that they may never see each other again, and Lee was reminded of why he did this job. It wasn't for the money, although it did pay well; but it had never been for the money. He just wanted to reunite people with their loved ones, as he hoped – one day – to be reunited with his wife and daughter, in the next life.

"So, you gonna get us out of here or what?" Harwood asked.

"You had enough?" Lee asked. "Some of your friends out there want to stay."

"Yeah," the young professor agreed, "I bet they do. They can get a bit obsessive like that. As for me, I think the stress has almost killed me already, you know? I belong in a lab, not out in the field. Man, when these guys picked us up, and killed those two people with us,

I'd never felt so sick in my life. So, those other guys can stay here if they want. Me, I'm going home. They can send stuff back for me to have a look at in the lab, you know."

Lee nodded in understanding. Not everyone was cut out for the rough stuff, and kudos to this kid for admitting it to himself. The dangerous ones were the people who tried to be something they weren't, now *they* were the ones who got themselves into trouble.

"Anyway, I've not decided what I'm going to do yet," Lee said. "I'll wait to send a message through to President Dunford, I guess. The job was to take everyone back, so I'll see what he says and take it from there."

"I can't believe he hired someone to find us," Harwood said in wonder.

"Not just him," Lee said. "Bakula and Darrow were in on it too."

"Makes sense," Harwood said, nodding. "Basically, they're the only people who knew about this expedition. All real hush-hush, for obvious reasons. Couldn't even tell our families about it, not all the details, anyway. Probably broke their hearts to tell *you* about it."

"Yeah," Lee said, "I think it did."

Lee looked back at the girl on the floor, wondering if it was worth waking her to give her the watch. "How's she doing?" he asked Harwood.

"Oh, she's better. Came down bad with it just yesterday. Thought she was gonna die at first to be honest, but they gave her some sort of home brew medicine, with that crazy orchid in it, and now she's doing a lot better."

"And you?"

Harwood looked down at his ankle and shrugged. "I guess the flower's just for illness and disease," he said. "Cos I've had some, and this thing *still* hurts like a sonofabitch."

Lee laughed. "Yeah," he said. "Still, nothing's perfect, right?"

Harwood laughed too. "So, what's the plan, anyway?"

Lee told him the outline, and Harwood nodded as he listened. "Well, hopefully Lisa here will be okay by tomorrow, if things get organized that fast. But Eva and I are gonna need some help. Even getting down from this damn treehouse is gonna be tough."

"You're not wrong there," Lee said, looking down at Lisa once more and deciding to let her sleep. She was going to need her strength.

Instead, he knelt down and removed the watch from his wrist, instantly missing the solid weight, and pushed in into her hands. She pulled it in to her tightly, like a child clutching a teddy bear, and Lee smiled. Let her wake with it, he thought. Let it be a nice surprise for her.

"You want to come for dinner?" Lee asked. "I think she's out for the count, you might as well come and join the rest of us."

Harwood smiled. "Yeah," he said, "why not? Just give me a hand, will you?"

THE EXTRACTOR

Lee went and bent in front of him, letting him loop an arm around his shoulder and hoisting him gently to his feet.

"Practice for tomorrow's extraction," Lee said with a smile, as they started moving slowly from the hut.

Harwood stumbled, cursed in pain, and then laughed. "Yeah," he said. "I think we're gonna need it."

Chapter Three

"Looks like a drugs lab got burned up last night," said Ryan Millhouse as Daniel Forster strolled into the ops room.

"Where did you get that from?" Forster asked. "Rodrigues?"

"No," Millhouse replied, "I don't even think Rodrigues knows about it yet. I'm plugged into a few of the networks the gangs use, I thought it would be a good idea, in case they came across the same guys we're looking for, you know?"

"Good thinking," Forster said, sitting down on a swivel office chair near Millhouse. "You think it's connected?"

"One man did it," the intel specialist replied, "*alone*. Took out five armed men empty-handed in the forest, then another *twelve* back at the lab. Kicked the hell out of them, spent the night in their bunkhouse, then blew the place to hell the next morning."

"That's gotta be John Lee," Forster said, before

whistling in admiration. "Damn, that guy's good. The cartel must be pissed."

"It is," Millhouse advised. "They're after blood, they just don't know whose."

"Hmm," Forster thought, wondering if he could somehow use their anger to his advantage. "Can we –"

A bleeping on Millhouse's system stopped Forster short, and the younger man checked it, verified it, then smiled widely and turned to his boss. "We've got them," he said.

Forster felt his pulse rise, his heart rate increase. "Which source?"

"Source Delta," Millhouse said, and Forster smiled too. "Perfect." It was the best of the multiple sources that might possibly have given them a location.

"Are we waiting for corroboration?"

Forster paused, thinking. Other sources might provide other information, such as exactly who was there, but Forster knew that such confirmation might never come. They had a lead, and his gut told him to act on it, and act on it immediately. "We have a precise target?" he asked.

"We do," Millhouse said, tapping a point on the screen of his computer, which displayed a large-scale satellite map of the area. "Right there."

Forster nodded. "Jack!" he called. "Get the chopper running. We're going hunting."

"What's wrong?" Hartman asked Phoenix, as she let out a yelp of nervous shock, sat behind her computer screen.

"I've got reports of sightings of a US Black Hawk chopper, leaving Feijó within the last hour."

"You're kidding," Hartman said, leaping to his feet and joining her at the console.

"I'm not," she said.

"You think it belongs to Apex?"

"It's got to."

"But how the hell did they get one? It's on the US munitions list for ITAR, isn't it?" ITAR was the International Traffic in Arms Regulations, and existed to stop the sale of military-grade equipment to non-authorized buyers.

"I guess someone felt they were an acceptable customer," Phoenix said, typing away furiously on her keyboard. "Yep," she said eventually, "their inventory shows *four* of them in total. All above-board, with end-user certificates."

"Damn. But there's only one around here, right?"

"Looks like," Phoenix said.

"So, where are they headed?"

"I don't know for sure," Phoenix said. "But they're going in John's direction."

"Damn."

"We're a lot closer than they are," Phoenix said, deep in thought.

"Closer to where?"

"The border. That's where John was headed, and I'm sure that's where these assholes are headed, too."

"Maybe," Hartman allowed.

"I know it. Wake Silva up," Phoenix said suddenly, thinking about the helicopter she'd managed to source earlier that day for the extraction, and which was ready and waiting for them. "And let's see if he can fly that damn chopper like he claims he can. And Markus?"

"Yeah?"

"Grab your rifle, too."

Chapter Four

"Well, look who it is," Gale said with a smile as Lisa Garfield walked slowly off the bridge and onto the dining platform. Dinner had long since finished, but most people – tribespeople and researchers alike – had now moved onto the palm wine, a particularly potent local concoction, and the smoking pipes.

Lee had abstained from both, but was enjoying the conversation, and was even beginning to pick up a few words of the tribal language. One of the things he'd picked up from following his diplomat father around the world as a kid, was a natural affinity for learning languages. He wasn't perfect in any of them, but was fluent in a couple, and conversational in quite a number.

"Hi guys," she said, and Lee was surprised that she'd had dysentery the day before; she didn't look terrific, but she looked a long way from death's door, and Lee could only suppose that the orchid had something to do with it.

He was holding one now, the stem a dark green like

the forest leaves among which it grew, the petals a rich, deep purple. It was a curious-looking flower, and Lee found it hard to believe that such an innocuous little thing could be so powerful. He looked from the flower, to Lisa, then back again, and marveled at the miracle of nature. There was, he knew, more out there in the world that we didn't know about, than that we did, and the thought humbled him.

"How are you feeling?" Jake asked.

"Better," she said. "Much better, thanks. But I found this watch with me when I woke up," she said, holding it up for everyone to see. "Who put it there?"

"It was me," Lee said. "I thought about waking you to give it to you, but it looked like you needed your sleep."

"Who are you?" Lisa asked.

"He's come to take us home," Gale explained. "Hired by Dunford and the others."

"Yeah," she said, sitting down with the group and looking at Lee. "But why the watch? What does it mean?"

"It's from Sylvia," he said, not knowing how much to say, how much the others knew about her relationship with the professor. "The watch you gave her."

The confusion on her face was obvious, like when he'd asked the drug runners where the researchers were – it was as if being confronted by the completely unknown. A cold shiver ran down his spine.

"I don't know what you're talking about," Lisa said.

"You had it engraved," Lee persisted, his head starting to throb now, the walls of his world squeezing inward. "Read it."

"I've read it," Lisa said, "and I still don't understand. Is it some sort of joke?"

Lee's heart stopped in his chest as realization started to dawn on him. She really *hadn't* seen it before.

Which could only mean . . .

He leaped up and raced toward her, shoving the flower he'd been looking at into the cargo pocket of his pants as he went. "Show me that watch," he said, nearly ripping it out of her hands.

He'd never really examined it before, had considered it someone else's property; he'd just been using his wrist to transport it here. But now he examined it, he was almost sick.

And then he heard it, far off in the distance but recognizable all the same.

A helicopter, coming this way.

A Black Hawk.

Which meant 7.62mm machine guns and miniguns, .50in Gatling guns, 70mm Hydra rockets, Hellfire laser-guided missiles and Stinger air-to-air missiles.

And maybe a whole bunch of commandos, armed to the teeth.

He took the watch, with its locator beacon – possibly activated by Lisa Garfield's fingerprint – and ran to the side of the platform, where he hurled it as far away into the rainforest as he could.

"Move!" he shouted to everyone at the top of his

voice. "Everybody, move, now!"

Forster scanned the dark canopy beneath them as they flew low over the rainforest, looking for any sign of life.

"We're nearly there?" he asked Lightfoot, who was up front with his co-pilot.

"Yes, sir," Lightfoot answered. "We're gonna be right over it real soon."

Forster could see nothing out of the windows, nothing through the regular monitors – and, for the time being at least, nothing through the night vision and thermal scopes.

"Wait a minute," he said, pointing to the thermal screen. "What's that?"

Lightfoot looked, and nodded. "Heat signature confirmed," he said. "Looks like flame, dead ahead. Damn, that canopy must be thick, to hide it like that."

"We've got movement," Forster said next, as human images started to appear on the thermal scope, running wildly in all directions. It looked like they'd heard the chopper coming, and decided it was bad news.

Which it most decidedly was.

"They're high up," Lightfoot said. "It's weird, like they're just under the canopy."

"Treehouses maybe," Forster said with a smile. "Safe from the ground maybe. But definitely not from us." The smile turned to a grin. "Open fire."

Chapter Five

The first set of rounds tore through the rainforest canopy like a swarm of angry hornets, blasting the tops of the trees to pieces.

Lee dove for cover, taking three villagers down with him, covering them with his body as the bullets raged overhead.

The research team was scared, hardly able to move with the fear; but the villagers were terrified, never having seen or heard anything like it in their lives. It was an attack from Heaven itself, and set them into wild panic. They were suddenly running everywhere, and as the chopper passed back and forth on its strafing runs, rounds chopping down ever closer, the first people started to get hit, 7.62 and .50 rounds blasting them apart like leaves; blood, bone and tissue was sprayed around the walkways and huts, and the scene was a nightmarish, surreal bloodbath that Lee wondered if they could ever escape from.

"Get down onto the forest floor!" he yelled above

the hail of machinegun fire. "Gail! Tell the villagers to leave the trees, to get down to the ground!"

He looked around the area, trying to find her, darkness of the night punctuated by the startling muzzle blasts of the chopper's guns.

Then he spotted her at the other side of the platform, hugging the floor, head down. "Gale!" Lee called. "Come on, snap out of it! Tell these villagers to get down off the trees!"

Her head raised tentatively, and she nodded; was about to call out, then stopped as a local woman was hit in the chest by a .50in round, her entire back blasted out across the dining platform, covering it in hot, sticky, black blood. Gale muffled a scream and got her head back down.

Dammit.

He got up into a crouch, tapping the three villagers below him and pointing in the direction of the climbing platform he'd ascended yesterday, then pointing downwards, hoping they would get the idea; they nodded and started crawling in that direction, while Lee began to crawl the opposite way, toward Gale.

He passed the other members of the research team as he went, all clinging to the floor for dear life. "Guys!" he called out. "Americans! Listen to me – your only chance is to get to the forest floor. It's eighty feet down, and the bullets won't penetrate down that far." Well, he thought, not as powerfully, anyway. "You need to climb down, now. Get moving!"

He watched as they all reluctantly started crawling,

even Jake and Eva with their injuries. The only one not stirring, Lee noticed in the dark, was Stephen; and when Lee crawled over to him to help, he could see why – the top of the man's skull had been ripped off, and his brain was leaking out onto the timber floor.

He turned and saw Gale crawling toward the climbing platform. "No," he hissed. "Not you. You've got to help me warn these people. Tell them to get down from the village." Lee looked across and saw the first people, in the dark distance, begin to ease themselves off the climbing platform and onto the vines that would take them downward; and then he looked back to the rest of the village, getting torn to pieces as the tribespeople continued to run in wild panic. "Come on!"

Slowly, reluctantly, Gale nodded her head, and Lee took her hand as they crawled further into the village. "There!" Lee said. "That's the chief, call him!"

Gale did as she was told, and the chief turned to them; Lee beckoned him over and – dazed and confused – the man stumbled in their direction, hot rounds missing him by mere inches.

Lee gestured for the man to get down, and he did, hunkering down on his hands and knees. "Gale," he said steadily, trying to keep everyone calm even as the minigun tore apart the wood structure around them, "tell him to get his people down into the forest. They need to get to ground level, and then run. Okay? Multiple directions. And make sure he tells them to take weapons."

"W . . . Why?" Gale stuttered, but he didn't want to scare her by saying it was in case the commandos followed them down.

"Just tell him," Lee said.

"I can't believe this is happening, I can't, I can't, who's doing this, who are they, who –"

"*Gale*," Lee said sharply. "Get a grip of yourself and do what I say. *Now*."

She nodded slowly, gathered herself, and translated. The chief looked at her with quizzical eyes, asked questions, and a debate ensued that ended quickly with a curt nod of the chief's head.

"Okay," she whispered. "He'll tell them."

"Good," Lee said. "Now let's move." He didn't want to worry her by saying that they might launch missiles at them next.

The air was filled with the acrid stench of gun smoke and human fear, the sound of rotor blades, gunfire and screaming almost deafening. But Lee still saw and heard the chief when he walked boldly out onto the main walkway, climbed up onto the post to stand tall, and addressed his villagers. He shouted out to them, and they stopped and listened, respect for the chief overriding – for a few precious moments, at least – their terror.

Bullets flew around the man as he shouted out to his people, but he remained miraculously unharmed; and then the people began to move, less panicked now, to the edges of huts and platforms, throwing off vines and doing as he'd instructed.

And then Lee noticed the chief collapse in pain, and realized he'd been hit all along, had merely put on a brave face for his people, and Lee was up and running toward him, catching him just before he toppled the wrong way over the bridge. He dragged him inside a hut as the chopper made another strafing run, and this time the missiles started to come, huts and platforms and walkways incinerated by the Hellfires, noise and destruction all around them, and Lee covered the man with his own body before pulling back to have a look at the damage the chief had sustained.

It was bad, through the lung, and he was already coughing up blood. Lee took off his shirt and rolled it into a ball, stuffing it against the wound before taking off his belt and cinching it tight around the chest, pulling the already blood-soaked shirt hard against the wound.

He dragged the man back across the platform, heading for the vines. He saw Gale ahead of him, disappearing over the side, and felt relieved that five members of the team seemed to have made it, at least.

He shrugged the chief onto his shoulders in a fireman's carry as he reached the edge, the world exploding around him, and he looked over and saw people climbing down below him. He swung onto a vine, holding firmly onto it with one hand while the other fed through the chief's legs before taking its grip on the vine.

And then, planting his boots against the trunk as the annihilation of the village continued around him, he began the treacherous descent.

Chapter Six

"Want me to take another run?" Lightfoot asked.

Forster used the thermal and night vision scopes to monitor the damage done so far. "No," he said. "I think it's time we put boots on the ground, don't you? Take us into a hover."

He could see that the people were trying to get out of the canopy now, to take their chances on the rainforest floor.

If Forster and his guys moved fast enough, the researchers and villagers might have a nice little surprise waiting for them when they landed.

"Come on guys," he said, as he moved into the main troop area. "Let's get down there."

It started to rain when Lee was halfway down the vine, a storm that came out of nowhere, obscuring everything, the noise of the torrential downpour almost drowning out the sound of the rotors above him.

He thought the explosions had stopped now, and

the gunfire; and if he wasn't mistaken, the chopper seemed to be hovering in one spot. Which could only mean . . .

Damn.

They were coming down, and he knew they'd be fast-roping to the forest floor, maybe quicker than Lee would get there himself.

"*Latan*," Lee whispered urgently to the chief, whose head lay near to his own. "*Latan.*"

It was one of the only words he knew in the tribal language.

It meant *fight*.

He needed the chief to tell his people. Fighting was the only chance they had.

"Latan," he repeated, like a mantra. "Latan, latan, latan –"

"*Latan!*" he heard the chief shout then, voice filled with power. He shouted more words at his people, the sound penetrating the rain and rotor blades, inciting the villagers to action.

And then he stopped abruptly, filled with a hacking cough that spilled thick, black blood over Lee's shoulder and chest; and then Lee felt the weight change, the body sag, and he knew the man was dead.

He heard the familiar sound of fast-roping next, heavy workman's gloves sliding down a thick braided rope suspended from the Black Hawk above.

He realized there were probably two ropes, one on each side of the helicopter, and he wondered helplessly how many mercenary killers were coming.

They must have been so close to him, to hear them over the rain, and he turned his head, saw the first man pass him on the way down, already firing at the people below with his submachine gun.

They were still twenty feet from the forest floor, but Lee no longer cared; he dropped the body of the village chief straight down, watching as the first man got hit by the dead body and knocked off the rope, falling helplessly to the floor. But before they hit, Lee was already jumping, knowing that the spacing was typically three meters between men – the perfect distance to allow the first to land and move safely out of the way before the next man came.

Sure enough, Lee contacted the second man almost immediately, intercepting him as he descended, knocking him clear of the thick rope. He grabbed hold tight and, as they fell, saw the commando wore NVGs; they'd be able to pick out the good guys as clear as day, and it would be a turkey shoot for these pros. The least he could do, he figured, was to take out one of them.

He kept on top of the man as he landed, crushing him underneath his own body, the unfortunate commando cushioning Lee's own fall.

Lee groaned in pain, but jumped up and raced ahead, back to the rope, just as the third man arrived. Lee swept the gun aside and kicked the man in the face, driving the goggles hard back into the guy's eyes, making him scream underneath the black combat mask he wore. He dropped to the rain-soaked ground, and Lee struck him in the side of the neck with the edge of his hand, before looking up and seeing the muzzle of an HK MP7 coming straight down toward him. But he ignored it and grabbed the end of the rope, pulling it violently one way, and then the other, the trigger pulled but the bullets going wide, the body falling soon after. It landed right next to him and Lee kicked the man in the chest, then the head, even as he continued to swing the big, heavy rope, each oscillation getting larger and larger, until the men above him – four that he could count – began to lose their grip, and fall from the sky, landing around him in pained heaps, dark puddles splashing around their injured bodies.

Lee heard gunfire from his left, knew that the other rope's team must have landed okay, and he turned and watched as they worked their way into the forest, muzzle flashes illuminating the horrendous sight of villagers – women and children – being gunned down in cold blood.

He heard movement nearby, saw one of the commandos who had fallen try to get up, to get his MP7 aimed; Lee was about to pounce, when suddenly, the man's head was smashed apart, a villager with a heavy club right there, screaming at the commando in the rain. And then the other fallen commandos were attacked by the villagers, with clubs, spears, arrows, hands, feet and teeth; they set upon the men with utter savagery, and Lee turned away, and ran toward the men who'd descended the other rope, to try and stop the massacre.

But then *they* started to go down, too; and through the pouring rain, Lee saw arrows sticking out of throats, spears running through ribs and chest and legs.

Latan.

The villagers were fighting back.

Just then, Lee saw Gale on the flooded ground, and he bent to her. "Are you okay?" he yelled.

She nodded, hardly able to speak. "Ye . . . Yes!"

"Get your team together," he told her. "And as many of the villagers as you can."

"Why?" she asked, eyes wide.

Lee pointed to the helicopter above them. "Because we're hitching a lift home."

CHAPTER SEVEN

By the time Lee reached the chopper, his arms were burning in pain. Those thick ropes were, he reflected, definitely easier to fast-rope down than they were to climb up, especially when there was more than a hundred feet to climb, in the pouring rain.

But he got there eventually, careful as he reached the open doorway; he could sense that someone was there.

Using what little strength he had left in his arms, he swung himself up and inside, kicking out with both feet as he went, scything the legs out from under the person who waited there. The man went down, and Lee scrambled aboard, elbowing him in the face as he tried to get back up.

Lee's body was hit then by a second man, presumably the one monitoring the rope at the opposite door, and he felt himself being propelled back toward the open space behind him. He dropped suddenly, planting a foot in the guy's stomach as he sat down and turning him over his head, straight out of the open door.

Instinctively, Lee spun around, onto his front, anchoring his feet inside, and reached out his hand for the falling man, who reached up with his own, panic in his eyes as he fell. Lee was scared he was too late, but then the man's hand clamped around his own, and he hauled him back up, into the chopper. The man started to thank him, but Lee cut him off with a headbutt that knocked him out cold. After all, just because Lee didn't want to kill him, didn't mean he wanted the guy left awake.

Lee's attention turned again then, as he saw the co-pilot coming out of the cockpit, aiming a Glock 9mm at him. Lee saw flak vests on the seats nearby – an old-school habit to help protect from incoming fire from the ground – and he grabbed one and held it up in front of him as he walked forward, feeling the impact as the vest absorbed the first shot, and then the second. There wasn't a third, as Lee gauged his distance and kicked the co-pilot in the gut, doubling him over; and then Lee knocked the gun aside, and slammed the vest down hard onto the back of his head. The guy collapsed to the floor, out for the count.

The next moment, Lee was in the cockpit, the co-pilot's pistol to the pilot's head. "Don't even think about moving this thing," Lee said. "Just keep it nice and steady, okay?"

The man ignored him, but did as he was told, obviously not knowing that Lee had no intention of using the gun.

Lee could no longer hear gunfire from down below, and he peered forward at the monitors, saw that the crazed, frantic movement had stopped. There were still bodies everywhere, but also plenty of moving ones.

Lee reached forward and activated the loudspeakers. "Gale," he spoke into the PA system. "We've got our ride out of here. Please start making everyone form an orderly queue for boarding."

Chapter Eight

The boarding process wasn't nearly as easy as he'd have liked it. The able-bodied came up the rope first, those best able to climb by themselves; the rest had to be hauled up by hand, which was both painful and exhausting, with the very real fear ever present that people's grip would fail them, and they'd plummet back down to the forest floor below.

But mercifully, that didn't happen, and even the injured managed to make it onboard. Through the PA, he'd asked Gale and whoever else was able to verify the numbers of dead, and make sure nobody else could be saved; if anyone down there was still breathing, Lee wanted them brought up to the chopper.

As it was, there were four surviving members of the research team. Sadly, Jake Harwood hadn't made it, shot through the heart with an MP7. But Lee made sure the body was on board, ready for burial back home. He'd also retrieved the body of Stephen Roberts from the village.

THE EXTRACTOR

There were also ten villagers onboard, which stretched capacity to well beyond maximum; but where there was a will, there was a way, and Lee managed to find the space for them.

Between the village and the ground, there were an estimated two dozen tribespeople dead; and with ten onboard, that meant that either there were sixteen or so more dead bodies that hadn't been found, or several of them had managed to escape into the forest. Lee liked to think it was the latter.

The Black Hawk full, Lee cut the ropes away and signaled the pilot – who was now under the careful watch of Greg Karlson – to come out of the hover and start the flight back to civilization.

"Phoenix," Silva said from the pilot seat of the civilian freight helicopter, "we've got contact."

Phoenix poked her head into the cockpit and looked at the radio. "John?" she said. "is that you?"

"John's with us," came the answer from an unfamiliar voice. "But he's busy looking after the injured."

Her blood ran cold with those words – 'the injured'. "Is the research team safe?" she asked.

"Four out of six," the voice said. "Which is a whole hell of a lot better than it would have been if John hadn't been there. I'm one of them, Greg Karlson."

"Is that your helicopter on our radar?"

"Yeah," Karlson replied, "that's us. Now, can you start arranging somewhere to go for medical care? Some of us are bust up real bad. There are ten survivors from the village too."

"I'll see what I can do," Phoenix said, happy beyond belief that John was alive and safe. She didn't know how he'd managed it, but was glad that he had.

Silva, to his credit, had tried to make it there on time, but the Black Hawk was a lot faster, and had already been in the air for some time, and they'd never really had a chance.

She turned to Silva. "Okay," she said, "let's get back to Cruzeiro."

She just hoped it had a decent hospital.

Diego Marcelles was pissed. One drug lab destroyed meant over a million in lost income a month, in US dollars. Maybe more.

Was it the US military? Those sonsofbitches were always causing problems. Well, he thought as he smoked a cigar, he had ways of dealing with *them*.

He radioed his men, as he stood looking at the ruins of the cocaine lab. "Are you in position?" he asked them.

"Yes," came the reply.

"Good. If you see something, tell me. Wait for my word, you understand?"

He got confirmation, and smiled to himself. From their positions in the high ground, they would spot those choppers from a long way out, if they returned the same way they'd come.

And then the Yankees would learn *not* to piss off

THE EXTRACTOR

Diego Marcelles.

Chapter Nine

"What the hell was that?" Phoenix asked, as the radar screen lit up like Christmas.

Silva looked at her, eyes sorry. "Not good. *Not* good."

"What the hell *is* it?"

"It's a damn missile," Hartman said from behind her, as he peered at the instruments. "And it's aimed right at that Black Hawk."

Phoenix sagged in her chair. "Oh no," she whispered. "Oh no."

Lee felt the aircraft lurch to one side, and knew the pilot had gone into evasive maneuvers; the IV from the onboard medical kit that he'd just inserted into the arm of a gunshot victim from the tribe burst out, blood and fluid spurting wildly all over the cabin.

What the hell?

And then he heard it, the telltale, high-pitched screech of a Stinger surface-to-air missile, closing in fast.

Too fast.

"Brace yourselves!" he called out.

Damn, he thought, *what next?*

Lightfoot wasn't flying the crew he was supposed to be flying, but he knew if the Stinger hit, he'd die just the same; and so he put everything he had into avoiding it.

He had no idea where it had come from, but it had to be close, too close for active countermeasures to kick in, and he was left with trying to move the large helicopter out of the way of the agile little missile; but it was too little, too late, and he knew it was only a matter of time before . . .

"It's hit!" Silva cried out, and Phoenix almost cried out as she watched the impact on the radar.

"Get us over there," she told him. "*Now*."

Lee felt the impact, waited for the chopper to explode; but when it didn't, he knew the pilot had turned them enough, just enough, to take the shot right at the rear.

It meant the strike wasn't fatal, bless him, but it also meant the rear rotor was taken out, and the chopper started to pitch and dive and spin, and Lee wondered if the crash that would inevitably follow might kill them all anyway.

"It's a hit!" Pedro Gonzales called into the radio. "I got the bastard, I got him!"

"Well done, Pedro," the voice of Diego Marcelles

came back to him. "Is it destroyed?"

Gonzales watched as the tail section leaked smoke and flame, sending the craft into a spin that took it over the treetops and over the horizon, beyond his eyeline. He waited a few moments more, moments that seemed to last forever.

And then, in reward for his patience, he could actually feel the impact rock the ground even from this distance, could hear the unhappy scarp and thud of heavy metal impacting the ground, and he smiled broadly.

"Yes, *Padrón*," Gonzales said happily. "It is destroyed."

Chapter Ten

Whoever the guy at the wheel was, Lee decided, he was an incredible pilot; despite being hit and being thrust into a flat spin from which there might have been no hope of recovery, the guy had managed to keep the Black Hawk aloft for long enough to avoid the trees, until he found a river and made a controlled crash-landing in that.

The impact had still been enough to rattle the teeth and – from the screams of pain around him – maybe even enough to break a few bones, but the water had absorbed a lot of it, and they were all now shaken and injured, rather than dead.

He started to rally everyone together, to get them off the chopper before it blew; and slowly, the passengers started to drag themselves into the water, swimming or wading to shore.

Lee heard the sound of another chopper and looked up, saw a freight helicopter hovering above the scene, coming in for a tight landing in a clearing by the riverbank.

Damn, he'd never been so pleased to see Phoenix in his life.

The villagers, talking among themselves, had clearly had enough though, and started to race away to the other bank from where the helicopter had landed, and where Lee and the research team were headed, even dragging their injured away with them.

Lee watched as Gale and Lisa started off after them, oblivious to the danger they were in, calling to them, presumably begging them to come back. But they had had their fill of the modern world, and Lee couldn't blame them. Being attacked once was bad enough, but twice?

It was then that Lee realized that Greg hadn't emerged yet, and nor had the pilot. "Marcus!" Lee shouted to the big man. "Come and help me, would you?"

He watched as Hartman exited the chopper, M4 in his hands; and before his friend was with him, he already started to wade back out to the aircraft.

He pushed inside, saw the two bodies at the front, seemingly unconscious, heads rolled to the side, and he moved forward, checking for damage.

The pilot's face was a mess, and from the way his body was folded, it was clear that he had some broken ribs, in addition to a possible skull fracture.

Greg, on the other hand, was blood-free, although it looked as if his legs had been crushed by the front console, which had folded in on him.

"Grab the pilot," Lee told Marcus, who immediately slung the rifle and carefully unbuckled the man from his seat, pulling him out and taking him out of the chopper. "And then come back and help with this guy," Lee called after him, recognizing that he was going to need some assistance; the guy was jammed in tight, and getting him out was a two-man job at the least.

A few moments later, Marcus popped his head back through, immediately crawling into the cockpit and leaning into the console, trying to move it while Lee pulled Greg free.

"Do you want the good news or the bad news?" Hartman asked him as he strained against the console.

"Give me the good news first," Lee said. "I'm a positive kind of guy."

Hartman grunted, and Lee wasn't sure if it was supposed to be a laugh. "Well, the good news is, I got the pilot safely to shore. Eve's keeping an eye on him."

"Okay," Lee said. "And the bad?"

"There look to be a bunch of caimans, headed this way."

"You're kidding?" Lee asked.

"I'm afraid not, John. We need to hurry, or all three of us are gonna be a snack for those guys."

Hartman strained harder, and harder, the blood vessels in his eyeballs threatening to pop with the effort, and finally there was movement, and Lee pulled Karlson clear, falling with the guy in his arms back into the main cabin.

"Okay," said Hartman, "let's go."

"I'll take Karlson," Lee said. "You grab Roberts and Harwood." They might be dead, but he didn't want the caimans taking their bodies. They deserved a proper funeral, if possible.

"Right," Hartman said, grabbing the two bodies, one under each arm as he waded out into the river, hot on Lee's heels.

Lee glanced right, then left, and saw the caimans, maybe five or six of them in the dark, eyes twinkling in moonlight that had been revealed now the storm had finished and the clouds had cleared. They were swimming close, just a few yards away now; and then he heard the single gunshot from the cockpit of the freight helicopter, and a terrified scream.

Chapter Eleven

Lee dragged the body onto the shore, Hartman following, as they ended up next to Eva and the pilot.

"What the hell was that?" Hartman asked, and Lee shrugged his shoulders. Was Silva up to some kind of trick?

But then the dead body of Eduardo Silva was thrown from the chopper to land on the sandy riverbank, a single gunshot wound in the back of his head.

And then Phoenix emerged, an arm around her neck, a pistol to the side of her head.

Lee recognized the man stood behind her with the gun, from briefing files on Apex Security.

It was Daniel Forster, one of the most experienced – and ruthless – of the company's team leaders.

Forster had decided to stay in the Black Hawk instead of fast-roping in with the men; he wasn't sure if it was just luck, or some sort of hidden sixth sense that had made him back out at the last second, but he was glad he had – all of the men who *had* gone were dead now, with all manner of primitive weapons sticking out of them.

He had hidden under the rear seats when Lee had climbed up the ropes; not out of cowardice, but out of a desire to see the mission through to the end. If he'd just flown away in the Black Hawk, he would have been okay, but he wouldn't have fulfilled his end of the contract – a dead research team, as well as a destroyed village and an annihilated tribe. if he allowed the research team to board, however, and then came out, all guns blazing in the confined space, he would have nicely ticked all of the boxes.

But then that bleeding-heart hero Lee had dragged all sorts of people onboard, the injured and even the *dead*, damn him, and Forster had been so crammed in that he hadn't been able to move a muscle.

And some stupid sonofabitch had launched a *missile* at them, which hadn't been part of Forster's plan at all. But, always ready to make the best of things, he remained hidden – though in tremendous pain from the crash, his head spinning and surely with at *least* three broken ribs – and had bided his time until everyone was distracted, at which point he had slipped out of the chopper, climbed aboard the new one, shot Silva, and taken the girl hostage.

Now all he had to do was shoot the others, then escape in the freight helicopter. It wasn't as pretty as the Black Hawk, but it would certainly do.

And then, before he got back to his superiors, he could work out how to put a positive spin on the story of how this little operation had turned into a complete disaster.

"What do you want?" Lee asked him, hands up in placation in front of him, the guy only six feet away on the narrow bank. Even in the dark, of night, fresh and clear after the storm, he could see the callous determination in the man's eyes.

"I just want to go home," Forster said. "But to do that, I need the rest of the research team. Where are they?"

"Took off after the villagers," Lee said. "They could be anywhere by now."

He knew this wasn't true, though; he'd seen them just after the gunshot, coming back on the far side of the river, and had gestured for them to get down, to take cover. But Forster definitely didn't need to know that.

"You'll have to find them, I'm afraid," Forster said. "Or else the princess here gets it."

"*Don't*," Phoenix said, body jerking violently as she threw an elbow back into Forster's injured ribs, crumpling him in the middle, "call me 'princess'!"

Lee took the opportunity and rushed forward, grabbing the gun and raising it into the air as Phoenix jumped to safety. Forster pulled the trigger and the weapon discharged into the night sky; but then, seeing that Lee was unbalanced with his arms in the air and his feet lower down than his own, by the river bank, Forster charged forward, pushing Lee backward, until they both crashed into the river.

Lee felt the warm water all around him, and latched himself onto Forster, making sure he couldn't get away. He felt the man clawing at him, then a heavy hammer fist that struck him above the eye. Lee hit back, targeting the ribs that he'd seen were injured. Forster gasped, and then let his fingers scrape up Lee's face and into his eyes, digging them in hard, trying to gouge them out of his head.

Lee twisted and turned with the pain, could just make out that people were shouting from the bank at him, though he couldn't make out what they were saying, and he ground his fist into Forster's ribs again in a vain attempt to make him give up the eye-gouge.

And then there was a horrendous, terrible, horrifying scream, and the fingers went slack of their own accord and fell away from Lee's eyes.

And when he finally managed, through the pain, to open them, he wished he hadn't; for there in front of him, was Forster's head, half-swallowed by a caiman, the jaws wrapped around the upper portion of the skull, the huge teeth digging straight through the face. Even in the darkness, Lee could see the flash of Forster's left eye, in a gap between two of the teeth.

And then the fearsome animal dragged Forster down with it, back into the water, and Lee thought that he might just be next.

But then the sound of an M4 opened up, and Lee

watched in gratitude as the caimans scattered, swimming away from Hartman's expert shots.

He dragged himself onto the shore, pained and exhausted. "Tell Gale and Lisa to come on over," he whispered to Hartman. "And then let's get the hell out of here."

Twenty minutes later, they were airborne again, flying back to the relative safety of Cruzeiro do Sul. The chopper held Lee, Phoenix and Hartman, along with Gale, Eve, Lisa and Greg, with the dead bodies of Roberts, Harwood and Silva also making the trip.

Lee piloted the chopper, while Phoenix sat next to him in the co-pilot's seat, hand on his arm for comfort. Lee welcomed it.

"I can't believe what happened," Gale said, coming to sit near Lee. "What we discovered, what we *could* have discovered, all gone. Now all we're left with is dead bodies." She began to cry, and Eva held her.

"Dead bodies," Lee agreed, "yes. But also maybe something else."

"Like what?" Gale asked, almost beyond caring now, in a state where she believed that truly nothing good could ever happen.

Lee reached into the cargo pocket of his pants, and pulled out the purple orchid he had been studying earlier. It was damp and bedraggled, but very possibly the very last of its kind in the world.

"Like this," he said, to the incredulous gasps of the researchers, and then smiled widely. "Like this."

Epilogue

Chicago Tribune
University Heads Killed in Car Crash
By Saul Underwood

Two major academics, and pillars of the world-renowned University of Chicago were killed yesterday when the vehicle in which they were traveling was involved in a head-on collision with a truck.

Gregory J. Dunford was the university's president, and Thomas N. Bakula served as Dean of the Biological Sciences Division. It is believed they were traveling together to a meeting when the tragedy occurred.

The driver of the truck has not been identified, and several eyewitnesses state that someone escaped the cab and ran from the scene. The police are appealing for more witnesses, but early reports indicate that the truck might have been stolen.

In other tragic circumstances for the university, a team of six professors and doctoral students are all believed to have died during a plane crash in Brazil, where they were to have performed research into the immune systems of river fish in the Amazon.

"It is a dark week indeed for the university," said Professor Sylvia Darrow, who was known to have worked closely with Professor Bakula., and who helped organize the research expedition. "We have lost some of our key personnel, and I have lost some dear friends. It is a tragedy that is difficult to put into words."

Sylvia Darrow closed the newspaper, folded it, and put it on the seat beside her as the limousine ploughed slowly through the downtown traffic.

It *was* a tragedy, she thought; it really was. But it was a tragedy that had left her ten million dollars richer, for doing nothing more than passing on a dummy watch and doing a bit of play-acting.

Reports from Brazil seemed to indicate that *everyone* was dead – the research team, the tribe, the men of the hired security team, and John Lee himself. It was all a bit confusing, but it seemed that a local drug gang armed with SAMs had something to do with it. And now Dunford and Bakula were dead too, before they could start asking any awkward questions.

When she'd originally heard about the report from Guzman and organized the research mission, it had been with all good intentions; but as she'd discussed it – in disguised terms, of course – with certain people, she realized how much money could be generated by such a discovery.

And then she had been approached by a man who claimed to represent the world's top five or six pharmaceutical companies, whose combined value was worth over a *trillion* dollars. They had, somehow, caught hold of rumors surrounding this secretive research trip, and at first, she'd thought they might be offering to help fund the expedition; but it quickly became clear that this was something very, very different.

They were, the man had told her, *scared*. Terrified, actually, that the team would discover something. They knew that if their own company was the one to develop a product from the discovery – if there was one – then the rewards would be fabulous, undreamed-of. But if it was one of their competitors, then their own companies would be ruined. After all, who would need drugs to battle disease, if there *was* no disease? It was a scenario that was nightmarish to the management of these companies and – even if these rumors were just rumors – they had come together as one and decided that the danger was too great, that they must act.

She remembered her first meeting, when – after her initial thoughts about them offering to help fund the trip were proved false – she'd then assumed instead that she was just being warned off sending the team in the first place. But then it transpired that they wanted the team to go, they wanted the tribe to be found – and then they wanted it to be eradicated, wiped clear off the face of the earth.

The original plan was for the team to locate the tribe, send information back to the university – which Darrow would then feed back to her contact – and then for a "security team" to be sent to the given location for the "clean-up" operation.

The first offer of one million had already been tempting, but when she understood that some of her own people were going to die, she'd managed to bump the figure up to ten. Was it immoral to take the money? She didn't know, but what she did know was that ten million dollars *was* ten million dollars, and who could argue with that?

And then the plan had started to go wrong. The team had gone missing, and nobody had any idea where they were, or how to find them. Her contact told her that the companies he represented were considering sending in a larger force to raze the entire area – and just blame the resulting destruction on an underground explosion, possibly due to illegal, unauthorized oil prospectors. But then Tom Bakula had thought about hiring John Lee, after reading a piece on him in *Time* magazine.

And so the plan had been changed. Lee would go in, and – when he tracked them down and reported their location – the word would then be sent for the security team to move in. But Lee could never know what the real aim was, hence the subterfuge with the watch, which had been arranged by Darrow's contact. They had lifted Garfield's fingerprints from glasses found in her home, and created the mechanism by which to activate the beacon when she was found. The inscription on the back, Darrow had thought, was a nice little touch.

The security team was monitoring radar and communications at all times, and there were several methods they were relying on to find the lost researchers, but in the end, it was the watch that did it.

And now they were all dead – including Dunford and Bakula, who had been killed to tie up the loose ends; any potential "cure" for disease was lost forever; and Sylvia Darrow had ten million dollars in her bank account, a possible Deanship in the Biological Sciences Division coming her way, and the eternal gratitude of Big Pharma.

It was, she thought as she passed through the grey

city streets, good to be Sylvia Darrow. Yes, sir, it was good to be Sylvia.

Just then, her car rolled slowly to a halt by the side of the road. She looked out of her window, wondering what the problem was; they were nowhere near the hotel, where she was headed for her final meeting with her contact, the car having been sent to collect her by the big firms.

"Why are we stopping?" she asked the driver. "Where are we?"

The driver turned in his seat, taking off his chauffeur's cap and sunglasses, and Darrow's blood ran cold.

The driver was John Lee.

Then her head snapped around as the door opened next to her, and she almost cried out at the supposedly dead faces she saw there, climbing into the limousine next to her.

Gale Rhodes. Eva Turner. Lisa Garfield.

Up in the front, she watched as John Lee got out of the driving seat, and Greg Karlson climbed in to take the wheel.

She looked at the three women next to her, their faces hard, as Karlson pulled out into the traffic. She went for the door handle, but it was too late. Locked.

And then she saw something appear in Lisa Garfield's hands, something small and black, and then it touched her body and she felt herself convulsing in agony as the Taser shut down her nervous system.

"To Sylvia," Darrow heard Garfield say, just before

she lost consciousness. "*With love.*"

Lee strolled down the streets of Chicago, body still aching from his recent ordeal but already on the mend.

He didn't know what the remains of the research team were going to do with Sylvia Darrow, but it would be nothing the woman didn't deserve, he was sure.

He also wondered if they would ever manage to do anything with the solitary flower they had managed to bring home from the rainforest. He hoped they would; it would, at least, give meaning to the losses that had been incurred over the past few days, and honor the memory of the fallen.

Phoenix joined him from under the awning of a nearby shop, linking arms with him as they walked down the sidewalk, a twinkle in her eye, a smile on her face.

"Can I invite you for a drink?" she said, and John smiled back.

"Sure," he said. "Why not?"

The strolled together toward the nearest café, Phoenix's head buried in his shoulder, and he started to feel a vague sense of contentment.

Then he felt the cellphone buzzing in his pocket, and he fished it out. Phoenix looked at him with a raised eyebrow, as Lee checked the caller ID.

"It's Alex," he said.

"Oh, no," Phoenix said. "Don't answer it."

He paused, as the phone continued to ring. "It might be important," he said, to be met with a warning look; Phoenix obviously didn't want their little date to be interrupted, for any reason.

He answered anyway. "Alex," he said, "how are you?"

"Good thanks, John," Grayson replied. "Look, I'll cut to the chase. I've got another job for you."

Lee looked at Phoenix, who was still giving him that warning look, brow furrowed. He knew it was too soon after the last one, that he hadn't fully recovered, that he needed the break; and then he flashed back to Iraq, what he had done there, and then to images of his wife and daughter, what had happened to them, and made his mind up in an instant.

"Go ahead," he told her, ignoring Phoenix's pained expression. "I'm ready."

THE END

. . . but John Lee will return in THE EXTRACTOR – MISSION:OUTBACK, out May 2018!!!

ABOUT THE AUTHOR

J.T. Brannan is the author of the Amazon bestselling political thriller series featuring Mark Cole, as well as the high-concept thrillers ORIGIN (translated into eight languages in over thirty territories) and EXTINCTION (his latest all-action novel from Headline Publishing), in addition to the psychological crime thriller RED MOON RISING.

THE THOUSAND DOLLAR MAN – the first novel to feature his new hero, Colt Ryder – was nominated for the 2016 Killer Nashville Silver Falchion Award.

Currently serving in the British Army Reserves, J.T. Brannan is a former national Karate champion and bouncer.

He now writes full-time, and teaches martial arts in Harrogate, in the North of England, where he lives with his wife and two young children.

He is currently working on his next novel.

You can find him at www.jtbrannan.com and www.jtbrannanbooks.blogspot.com, on Twitter @JTBrannan_, on Facebook at jtbrannanbooks, and on Instagram @jtbrannan.

Also by the Author

The Colt Ryder series:
THE THOUSAND DOLLAR MAN
THE THOUSAND DOLLAR HUNT
THE THOUSAND DOLLAR ESCAPE
THE THOUSAND DOLLAR CONTRACT
THE THOUSAND DOLLAR BREAKOUT
THE THOUSAND DOLLAR MURDER
THE THOUSAND DOLLAR TEAM

The Mark Cole series:
STOP AT NOTHING
WHATEVER THE COST
BEYOND ALL LIMITS
NEVER SAY DIE
PLEDGE OF HONOR
THE LONE PATRIOT
AGAINST ALL ODDS

Alternative Mark Cole thriller:
SEVEN DAY HERO

Other Novels:
RED MOON RISING
ORIGIN
EXTINCTION
TIME QUEST

Printed in Great Britain
by Amazon